THERE CAN
ONLY BE *Secrets*

White Willow Press

ANDREA LEVESQUE

from the library of

ISBN 978-1-955208-14-7

Summary: After being pushed out of the elite secret society known as the Order of the Six for plotting to take them down, Harper Fontaine finds herself once again wrapped up in the allure of the Order's lethal mystery - this time, in New York City.

For my love, Jenna.

Contents

ONE

---◆—◆—◆---

"Harper?" Someone called my name. It was Valentina's mom, my almost new stepmother, searching for me in her white sundress at the bridal shower this past summer, unaware that her big day would be ruined by the blood of one of my oldest friends. And then she was there in a very different white dress, a much more important one. It was expensive and lavish, the kind that could only be owned by Newport's wealthiest. And then she was screaming.

And so was I. We all were. At least, that's what it seemed like to me. A blur of faces flashed before me as I felt my knees press hard on the pool's edge, the air escaping my throat with such fervor I wondered if it could somehow whirl away and turn back time.

"Harper!" The words floated in my direction, ricocheting throughout the space, the sound jumbled somehow. My head moved slowly through a fog, and it was Valentina, I thought, begging for me to notice her brother being pulled away in handcuffs. It was my dad, his voice heavy, crying for someone to notice me, to remove me from the gruesome scene, and pleading for Dom to be revived by the pounding of his palms on his chest. And then it was Nina, questions hanging between us, blame dripping from her eyes.

"Harper, did you hear me?"

The world shifted, and I found myself in my bedroom in my mom's apartment. I didn't speak, trying to recall what she'd just said. She sighed and put her hand to her forehead.

"I said, did you do any of your schoolwork today?" My mom nodded to my laptop, the dark pieces of hair that framed her face outside her sleek ponytail swishing with movement. No, it wasn't the sweltering month of June anymore, and I wasn't in Newport. It was September, and I was in New York, I reminded myself once again. I had to do that a lot these days. After what happened with Dom, it was hard to keep my mind on the present. And right now, that meant homeschooling.

My eyes drifted in the direction my mom was looking, my closed laptop collecting dust.

"Yeah," I lied. "I worked on a couple things."

My mother's brows furrowed together, catching my dishonesty but not calling me on it.

"Harper," she said, walking towards me and taking a seat on the edge of my bed. Her slender frame was light, barely dipping the plush comforter as she sat down. "I know you're having a hard time. It can't help that Nina isn't making an effort, but I was hoping allowing Valentina to live here would help make up for that. When your father suggested it, I wasn't sure at first, since coming back here was supposed to bring you a little normalcy, but she's been great. Don't you think so, honey?" My mother's head cocked to the side, noticing my distance.

Something in my brain shifted again, and I heard my name being called somewhere in the back of my mind.

"Hey," she said softly, and I felt her hand move to my leg, attempting to get my attention. The contact made me jump, and I came to, finding myself in a coffee shop on the Upper East Side. I blinked hard.

3

Valentina was standing over me, her hand pulled back like she'd touched a hot pan. She hadn't. She'd touched me, and snapped her arm back when I'd jumped, I realized. My heart pounded and I looked around, taking in the posh café with its round wooden tables and sleek countertop covered in a sparse arrangement of baked goods. There were large glass windows at the front, letting in light from the busy streets, the last remnants of summer drifting away as fashionable street-goers passed by in their brand new autumn pieces.

"Harper?" Valentina asked so softly I was sure no one heard it but me. She'd been the one calling my name, not my mother, not my dad, and not Nina. I wasn't in my bedroom; I'd been here the whole time. That conversation with my mother had happened hours ago.

I swallowed and pulled a chair out at my table, the metal feet making a loud scraping sound, grating on my ears. Valentina sat down slowly, her eyes never leaving my face. I couldn't look her in the eye, not when things like this happened. It felt too…vulnerable, like I was

4

doing her a disservice by living somewhere else in my brain when she was sitting right there.

"I'm sorry," I whispered, my eyes on the square napkin torn to shreds in my palm. I opened my hand and let the pieces sprinkle silently onto the floor.

"Another…?" Valentina didn't finish the sentence, probably worried even saying the word would send me back there. *Flashback*. She knew I knew what she meant.

"Yeah."

Her hand slipped into mine, her soft skin spreading warmth throughout my body this time and allowing me an ounce of comfort. Tears sprung behind my eyes, and I blinked them back quickly, hoping she wouldn't notice. Valentina did this to me. She made me feel safe. She made me feel loved. Because I *was* loved by her. And I wasn't sure I deserved it. But I would accept it, anyhow.

I pushed my drink toward her, the black coffee barely touched since I'd ordered it twenty minutes ago. "Here," I said. "You're probably exhausted. I know the commute from Rhode Island can be a bitch." I laughed a little, but it sounded forced.

Valentina offered me a small smile and took a large gulp of the warm liquid.

"It's really no big deal. If it means I get to spend time with both you and Adan, I'll do it every week."

I squeezed her hand. "You do, V."

She gave me a noncommittal laugh. "And if the tables were turned, I know you'd do the same."

I bit my lip. "How is Adan?"

"Fine." Valentina's cheeks tightened, and it clicked for the first time that she was holding something back. I blinked, trying to push the fog from my brain. What kind of girlfriend was I that I hadn't noticed something was up with V these past few months?

"V?" I asked, leaning toward her, a flash of the old me slipping into place as I became the caring girlfriend once again instead of the distant psychiatric patient I'd been acting like since the tragedy occurred.

Another hand landed on top of mine as Valentina cupped my palm in both of hers, assuring me she was telling me the truth. But she wasn't. "Really Harper, everything is totally fine. You know, Adan's not going to be amazing, but he's off house arrest now that the police determined there wasn't enough evidence to charge him. It's what you'd expect."

Rebecca, I thought. She got Adan off, as promised. So long as I stayed away from the Order and didn't cause trouble, we were all safe. For now.

"V, just tell me. I can handle it."

She dropped my hands and leaned back in her seat, picking up my coffee but not sipping it. Her cashmere cardigan draped open, revealing a fitted tank top that stopped at the hem of her mom jeans. "Can you?"

My chest tightened. There was no judgment in her voice, she was truly asking. But the implication stung, knowing that no, I hadn't been able to handle anything since Dom died. Not seeing Dom's family, my old friends, or anyone I used to know when I lived here. I couldn't manage going on any real dates with Valentina, or feeding myself properly without the help of my mom and V. Even the easy schoolwork Wellsley Prep had sent me to ensure I could finish high school and continue to name them on my resume, albeit as an online program, just didn't feel important. Because at the end of the day, nothing was anymore.

I gulped, my throat dry. "I can try." And I wanted to. I wanted to feel like myself again. This useless girl with no meaning in life was a waste of space, and I never imagined I'd be that way. My grandfather would be so crushed, had he lived to see this day.

There was silence, so I spoke again, pushing. "Really V, tell me what's going on. Maybe I can help. Let me try, okay?"

Her fingers traced the rim of the mug, silver rings clacking against one another, her eyes following the movement. "Well, the truth is..." I waited, and eventually Valentina continued. "Adan isn't speaking to me."

"What?"

Valentina pushed the cup forward and looked up at me, her eyes round with anticipation. "He hasn't this whole time." She lowered the cup to the table, her eyes still looking anywhere but at me.

"Adan blames me...for being found at the pool when Dom was—" She cleared her throat, not finishing the sentence. "Well anyway, he's right. It was my fault. I'm the one who lied to him about the time the wedding started to make sure he'd show up late. If

I hadn't done that and sent him on a wild goose chase for a piece of made-up jewelry in my bedroom, Adan would have been at the ceremony with everyone else, and he would never have been the one to find the body." I jumped a little at the comparison of Dom to the word *body*. Valentina cringed, realizing her mistake. I sighed. I hated that everyone had to walk on eggshells around me. I didn't want this. Dom didn't want this. But then again, I doubt he wanted a knife to the chest either, and here we were.

"You can't feel guilty for that, you couldn't have known."

Valentina's lips pressed together and she stared at me. "Do *you* feel guilty?" For Dom, I knew she meant. I was quiet. "Exactly," she continued. "So we all have our burdens to bear." Another silence stretched between us as I grappled for something encouraging to respond with. Luckily, Valentina spoke again, as if this exchange between us was the opening she'd been looking for for a long time.

"And that's not all. I think there's something he's not telling me. Something about what happened that day that he won't share."

I snapped my head in her direction. "How do you know?"

She sighed. "He's my twin brother. Of course I know. I just can't figure out what it is. This is more than just blaming me for what happened." She sighed, and I considered what I knew about Adan's situation. Of course there was something going on with him, that much was obvious. He was home all the time now, put on the same online program through Wellsley that Valentina and I were on in order to graduate. And he had to be, because it was clear through the sugar-coated morsels Valentina had shared over the last few months that Adan refused to leave the house entirely. That certainly meant school. And it occurred to me just now that maybe he hadn't even been leaving his room, either.

"There is something, but he won't tell me. He won't even talk to me. He won't really talk to anyone."

I pictured Valentina sitting in silence in Adan's room, or maybe knocking on his door and not getting a response. A sick, hollow feeling spread through my gut as I imagined the pain Valentina must be in every time she goes home. It was the same pain I had when I thought of Dom. It was the pain of loss.

The clinking of mugs and hissing of steam filtered towards us from behind the counter. I blocked out the noises and tried to focus, images of Adan in the pool and Dom's dead body trying to press their way to the forefront. *Dom's smile. His curly hair. The blood.* The sweet boy who I'd once helped with his math homework had been reduced to a mangled figure in my brain, forever covered in blood, never to be scrubbed away. I forced the images from my train of thought, the gears turning in my head, the mystery-solving girl from last year trying to claw her way to the surface.

"And…and your mom?" I asked, hesitating briefly. I should have asked about all this months ago. Valentina frowned.

"Why do you think she doesn't care that I'm practically living here now?"

Ah, so Macy was mad at her. Not surprising, the petty woman probably blamed all of us for ruining her wedding to my dad, though Adan least of all. He was her golden child these days, a victim in all this, which meant someone had to be the villain. With me gone, it was Valentina once again.

"Look," she said, pulling out her phone and attempting to exude an air of casualness. "Don't worry about it. He'll talk to me when he's ready. I get it. It's been a lot. Let's just try and focus on us right now, okay?" Her shoulders rose and fell, brushing off her concern.

I sat back in my seat, defeated. The sleeves of my sweatshirt hung low on my wrists, and I pulled at them, letting them cover my hands. It was still a bit too warm for the matching tracksuit I was wearing, but I didn't care, I just wanted to be comfortable.

A fixed point on the wall caught my focus as I stared off into space. I thought everything with the Order of the Six was over. Dom was dead, and so was my grandfather, Valentina's dad, and probably Jack Cunningham too, as far as I was concerned. He disappeared the moment his grandfather, Allastair, discovered his disobedience and hadn't surfaced since. Everyone who might actually know something and be able to help us was gone forever. I had the Order to thank for that.

But if there was more I didn't know about...I already had so many unanswered questions. Maybe leaving the whole thing alone wasn't the answer. Then again, no one had died in the months since the showdown between Rebecca and I on the beach that day. Either way, I couldn't help but get the feeling something was going on, something I should pay attention to.

A camera noise went off as Valentina snapped a photo of the fancy mug of coffee. In her typical hot girl fashion, I guessed she was posting the image to social media.

"Your mom mentioned something about going to lunch. Do you think you'll be up for it? It's totally fine if not, I was just thinking..." Valentina trailed off, her fingers going white as she gripped her phone hard, abruptly pulling the screen closer to her face.

"V?"

"I—I...wait, is this for real?"

I made a face, wishing she'd clue me into whatever was leaving her speechless. I almost stood up and walked behind my girlfriend to see what she was looking at, until she tore her gaze away from her screen and stared at me, a mix of awe and fear pricking across her face. My stomach dropped.

"What is it?"

"Harper, you're not going to believe this." Valentina's voice shook. Her once waist length hair now fell in even chunks below her collar bone as she leaned forward. V turned her phone towards me, revealing a tiny square image posted to a local fraternity. A tall brunette guy tossing a ball into a red solo cup filled the frame, his name tagged in the caption below. I squinted, trying to wrap my mind around the image.

"Is that—?"

"Jack Cunningham," V said, her voice low. "Jack is *alive*. And he's here, in New York. At Columbia. Like he was supposed to be all along." *But wasn't*, I thought. He *wasn't* at Columbia like Allastair and Rebecca said he was. He'd disappeared for over three months. Jack Cunningham had vanished from the face of the earth. Until now.

Which meant something *was* happening. Or, had happened at least. And it wouldn't be anything good. All this time I'd been operating on the assumption, however morbid, that Allastair Cunningham had killed his own grandson to protect the Order's secrets, the very ones Jack had risked exposing when he told his chapter—rather, our chapter—of the Order about the pirate Malloy's treasure. That secret had been kept for generations by the Cunningham family, only to be leaked by a pompous teenager in his search for notoriety. It was because of him that Valentina and I had uncovered so many of the Order's secrets and tried to take them down the day of the wedding. And it was because of that that I discovered my own family, the Fontaines, were the original owners of Rose Island, and descendants of Malloy and, most importantly, the true heirs to the Rose Island treasure.

Not that Allastair was aware I knew that part, of course. Not yet.

Now, with Jack alive and cast out of the Order, there was someone else who knew the true history of the Order of the Six, and beyond that, the deepest secrets of the Cunningham family. If I could get to him, if I could get him on my side, maybe I'd have a shot at getting the proof I needed to take down the Order. All this time I'd been compliant to Rebecca and Allastair's wishes, but there was a new Cunningham in the ring, and he lived just down the street. And he'd been burned by the same people I had.

Energy buzzed beneath my hands and feet, the excitement of this prospect filling me with life once again. Retribution was tangible, I decided. Now, I have a purpose. I could bring Dom the justice I swore I'd bring him the day he died. And it would take the old Harper to get it.

"We're not going to lunch today, Valentina." My eyes locked on hers, the same determination reflected on her face as on mine. "We're going to find Jack."

TWO

———◆—◆—◆———

"Sorry, what's the plan?" I asked, discreetly turning my head in Valentina's direction. We sat on a stone bench in the middle of the quad, manicured grass sprawled out in every direction around us.

"Well," Valentina pushed her 90's inspired sunglasses further up the bridge of her nose. She looked like she should be starring in *Cruel Intentions*, not attempting a stakeout on a college campus. "According to my Columbia source, Cunningham has class in that building at noon." She pointed a finger in the direction of a large brick building across from us, its entrance wide and stately. "So, in like, just a few minutes."

My eyes dropped to Valentina's ripped jeans and crop top, the entire look ridiculous on her, making her torso appear never-ending. "No, I'm talking about the wardrobe choice. It's not that I don't support you

17

trying something new, but I'm confused. We stopped home so you could change into clothes that don't fit you? That's definitely not Gucci. I didn't even know you owned stuff like that."

Valentina glanced subtly in my direction. "Harper, this is camouflage! I'm supposed to look like a college student. You know, blend in a little?" Her eyes cut to me again. "Which is why you need to stop staring at me! Do you want Jack to walk by and notice us? He might book it in the other direction or something! We need to take him by surprise."

"We're sitting on the same bench, wouldn't we know each other?"

Valentina huffed. "Maybe, maybe not. This is a university, people mingle all the time that don't know each other. And anyway, it doesn't matter!" Her voice was low. "We're just trying not to draw attention."

My eyes scanned the crowds of people making their way across campus. The crowd was littered with young people from all backgrounds, their wardrobes clean and fresh for the new year. Well, most of them, anyway.

I squinted. Heading this way, about thirty feet from us, was a tall guy with that same brown hair from the Instagram photo. *Jack.* I recognized his signature shiny loafers and crisp button-down shirt from almost every meeting I'd had with him. Before I could signal Valentina, she slid lower in her seat quickly and hissed, "There he is!"

I followed suit, slouching a bit more on my end too and keeping my head down. I pulled out my own sunglasses from my pocket and slipped them on, heart racing.

"Now what?"

Valentina glanced in my direction. "Let him get a little closer." Her gaze trailed across the scene in front of us and pointed in the direction of a small group of freshmen huddled together in some kind of tour group, broaching the building together. When they got close enough to the building that they were only feet from us, Valentina grabbed my elbow and pulled me to my feet, whisking me behind them. I tried to slow my breathing, but between keeping a tight pace behind the group and one eye on Jack, who was almost at the entrance, it was a losing battle.

"Let him go in first," V whispered in my ear, the feeling tingling my skin through my hair. The sensation sent a jolt of electricity through me, and with the adrenaline from our task at hand already pumping through my veins, I suddenly realized what I'd been missing out on these past few months. It was that spark that used to jump between us. I had the urge to forget what we were doing and pull Valentina into a kiss right there, my hands tight on her neck, lips warm, but I knew I couldn't. Later, I urged myself, I would try and bring back this feeling. I would let myself have it.

Jack stepped inside and we followed, the group in front of us disbursing slowly in different directions. If he turned around now he might notice us, but that would be okay. As long as we could corner him, we could force him to talk to us.

Just as we turned to follow Jack down an adjoining corridor, my eye caught on two broad men in expensive black suits. One of them wore sunglasses, despite being indoors, and their "Men in Black" appearance gave me pause. I slipped my own sunglasses on top of my head.

"Wait." I grabbed Valentina's elbow this time and steered us away from the corridor Jack had headed down.

"What are you doing?" Valentina asked, her brows knit together in confusion. "We have to stop him before he walks into class!"

I extended a subtle finger in the direction of the two suits, who had caught up to Jack and were now following about ten feet behind him. I let the warning in my chest linger, holding us back. "Look. Cunningham has a tail. That's new."

Our eyes met. *Trouble.* "Shit," Valentina cursed. "Order goons. They have to be, right? Who else would be tailing Jack?"

I pressed my body up against the wall and leaned my head back, eyes closing. "Of course Allastair is going to have Jack watched. Maybe he didn't have the heart to kill his own grandson after all, but you know he doesn't trust him. Whatever they did to him these past few months, it was definitely some kind of punishment or something. Insurance to be sure Jack would follow the rules again. I mean, right?" God, we were stupid to think we could just march right up to

Jack and ask for answers. He was still part of the most important family in the Order.

"Okay, okay. New plan." Valentina slipped her own sunglasses off and peered down the hallway. We watched a smattering of students lingering outside the classrooms, some making their way in slowly. "We catch him *after* class…we approach him in the mix of students so his bodyguards assume we're just other kids talking about homework or something. Obviously we can't let them see our faces in case they're instructed to like, keep an eye out for us or something, but I think we can do it."

I nodded. "Now's our chance. Ready?"

Valentina looped her arm through mine and we took a casual step behind a small cluster of students turning down the adjacent hallway. When we made it in front of the room Jack had walked into, we turned quickly and snuck inside, avoiding direct contact with the two bulky men intermittently scanning the hallway.

"Wow," Valentina whispered, her eyes surveying the massive classroom, probably one of the few large classes on a campus that usually boasts small class-to-student ratios.

"Well, this is certainly a change from Wellsley prep, huh?" I whispered to Valentina, leaning toward her. When I went to public school, the classrooms were pretty big. The diversity of the city was definitely reflected in the school district, and I considered now how different the white-washed, exclusive setup of our private school in Newport really was. I wondered if coming from a small place like Newport made even Columbia feel overwhelming to Valentina.

A quiet chatter filled the room as students moved about, taking their seats, catching up with old friends or attempting to make new ones. The professor rifled through some papers at his desk at the front of the classroom, preparing for the class's imminent start.

"Right there," I said quietly, pointing at Jack, who was taking his seat in the middle of the auditorium. Valentina tripped a little as I pushed her towards him, and I wondered if she was nervous. Just moments ago she was taking charge, totally comfortable with the cat and mouse game we were playing. Now that we'd changed arenas, however, it appeared she was forgetting just which furry mammal we were supposed to be.

Some last-minute students entered the room and squeezed behind us, forcing us to turn into the row Jack was sitting in. I tried to shoot V a panicked look, but she was staring straight at Jack. We weren't supposed to sit *near* Jack, we were just supposed to wait it out in the back of the room until the class ended. But at this point, we would already be within his range. Either we sat *next* to Jack and tried to get something out of him right away, or we could risk him seeing us before we wanted him to.

Valentina must have had the same thought, because the two of us slinked toward the empty seats on either side of our target, praying he didn't notice us yet. Something about her posture set off warning bells in my head. Her head wasn't in the game anymore. I knew, because that's how I'd been feeling for months. But too much was at stake here.

"Get it together V, remember why we're here. Focus," I said in her ear. "Think of your brother." She glanced back at me, acknowledgement in her eyes. With her usual confidence returning, she plopped casually into the empty seat on Jack's left, leaving the seat on his right open for me.

My chest thundered with anxiety, but I followed her lead and dropped in beside the guy whose family had single-handedly murdered my best friend just a few months ago. This wasn't just another college kid, I reminded myself. He was important.

And then he saw us. I expected him to protest, to ask us what we were doing there or to stand up and demand we leave, but he barely looked at us. Instead, Cunningham simply pulled his laptop from his strappy bag and opened it on his lap. Valentina and I stared at each other in confusion, then looked back at him. It was as if he hadn't seen us at all. But that was impossible; with little rearranging, Valentina and I would practically be in his lap.

"Jack," I whispered, leaning in toward him. He glanced in my direction, as if surprised I'd spoken to him. He raised one of his eyebrows, but there was nothing else on his face to distinguish what he was feeling besides confusion, and a little bit of...*annoyance*?

"Yes?"

"We need to talk."

He cocked his head. "I'm sorry, about what?"

I gawked, saliva stalling in my throat. Valentina, noticing my stumble, leaned in from the other side.

"We need to talk to you about the Order, Jack. It's important."

His head swiveled arrogantly in her direction, and he chuckled. "I think you're thinking of a different school, freshman. Columbia doesn't have a frat called the Order." This time, Valentina was at a loss for words, just in time for the class to settle into a quiet hush as the professor walked to the front of the room. My chest constricted. We were running out of time.

"Cunningham, this isn't a joke. We know the Order kicked you out. We know they did something to you. You've got to be pissed about the whole thing. Come on, let us help you. We've been through it too, and we're also pissed. Let's talk about this." My voice was low, but not low enough. I worried someone around us might hear, but this was too big. Even if they did hear me, they probably wouldn't know what we were talking about. And if Jack had a problem with it, maybe he'd agree to have this conversation more privately and we could finally get somewhere.

Jack scoffed, his attention shifting to the professor, who was discussing the chapter the class had been assigned for reading. We were losing him, I could tell.

"Don't you wanna get back at your sister?" V added, still leaning in closely to Jack's left shoulder.

Jack snickered. "I do hate my sister, but I was hardly aware that was common knowledge."

"If you'd just—" Before Valentina could finish her plea, a voice boomed from below us.

"Ladies, is there something more important than Psych 101 that you'd like to bring to our attention?"

I shrunk down in my seat, putting my hand over my eyes. I'd like to pipe up to the sexist teacher and say that it had actually been Valentina and *Jack* that had been talking, not me, not for a while at least, but I certainly wasn't going to. I watched Valentina glance over at Jack, whose smug expression let me know he wasn't planning on copping to causing the disturbance.

When neither of them said anything, the bald man spoke again. "You, with half a shirt on, stand up please." Pink spread across Valentina's face as she slowly rose to her feet. Her tall frame did nothing to

27

help her shy from the attention. *Oh god,* I thought, *we don't even go to this school.* "Would you care to enlighten the class on the function of the frontal lobe?"

She swallowed. "Well, uh, the frontal lobe is in charge of executive functioning. Decision making, that kind of thing." Her hand went to her elbow to cover her bare stomach. Uncertainty was a strange look on Valentina, and I wondered if this was what it was going to be like for her as a real college freshman. Maybe spending time in the big city with me was actually going to be good for her. The idea that I could have a positive impact on her, despite the pile of dog shit I'd pulled her into this past year, was an odd thought.

"Go on," the professor said, crossing his arms and settling deeper into his torso.

My eyes were intent on V, wondering if there was something I should be doing to help. The urge was odd. Valentina Vasquez rarely needed help with anything, but the tugging in my chest begged me to shield her from the embarrassment.

But she continued anyway, her gaze now firm on the man holding ground in the front of the room.

"Memory, attention, empathy. Self-control. It's responsible for those as well."

Wellsley Prep academics for the win. I was starting to understand why parents—the ones who could afford to at least—sent their kids to high level prep schools instead of public schools, like the ones I attended for most of my life. I wasn't sure I'd know how to answer any of these questions.

"Ah," Professor-Ego said, lifting a hand and waving it around. "Self control. Yes, that makes sense, doesn't it? Considering the frontal lobe doesn't finish developing until at least the age of 25, it's clear that some of you *would* have trouble with many of these things. Would you say that's something you're struggling with right now, Miss—?"

And that did it. Valentina's jaw hardened, her hip jutted out to the side and she leaned into it, once again becoming the girl who refused to take shit from anyone. That was the Valentina I knew and loved. Instead of answering his question, she lifted her own hand and waved it around, mirroring the professor's arrogance.

"Actually, no. I was thinking of *real-world* behaviors like drugs, or alcohol consumption. These are actually incredibly risky activities to take part in as an adolescent, which, yes, includes college students, if you understand the damage that's being done." A good-natured boo-ing spread around the room, but Valentina continued. "Until the brain reaches maturity, these behaviors can drastically impact frontal lobe development, doing permanent damage." She paused, crossing her arms. "I would think those matters would take priority in your teaching, Professor, unless, of course, you feel you spend enough time already on drugs and alcohol. It seems to me that might be the case, anyhow."

A collective *ooh* spread throughout the classroom, and Valentina took her seat. I was probably grimacing at the whole exchange, but no one was looking at me. Everyone was staring at Valentina.

"See me after class." Even from where I was sitting I could see the professor's eyes narrow, but he didn't call on Valentina or me for the entire duration of the hour after that. When the class was finally dismissed and the noisy chatter began again, Valentina and I leaned back into Jack as he packed up his things.

"Look, let's go find somewhere to talk, okay? We can't really do this in public," Valentina suggested.

"As amusing as you ladies are, I have somewhere I need to be," Jack said.

My hand went to his arm, vying for his attention in vain. "Jack, please. This is serious. For once in your life—"

"How do you know my name?" he asked, pompously flicking my hand off his arm. "And how do you know I have a sister? If this is some kind of fraternity hazing, they're going a little too far with this madness. I was told my spot was on lock and I didn't have to entertain this bullshit."

Valentina and I froze, dumbfounded. Jack stood up, swinging his bag around his shoulder and moving to step by Valentina. Before he could, she sprang into action and blocked his path in the slim auditorium row.

"Jack," she pleaded, her voice stern. "It's me. Valentina? The girl you grew up next to? This is a joke, right? We went to elementary school together, and high school, and...everything? Our parents forced us to dance at the middle school homecoming? If you're messing with us, it's really *not funny.*" Those last two words were hard and slow, as if this back and forth was starting to irritate her, which it certainly was.

"No," Jack said, pushing Valentina to the side with the back of his arm. "This *isn't* funny." Annoyance flashed in his eyes again, covering something I could almost see deeper inside—a hollowness paired with confusion.

"I've never seen either of you before in my life. If you don't leave me alone, I'll call my bodyguards in here to take you to campus security." With that, he side-stepped V and walked down the rest of the aisle, coolness exuding from him like it would from a celebrity, his crisp shirt and perfectly tousled hair making him appear entirely unbothered. Valentina and I just stood there, unsure what to do or what to say, even to each other. But one thing was for sure. Something had happened to Jack. And by the looks of it, we were royally screwed.

THREE

"Goddamnit!" A reverberating metal sound filled my ears as Valentina kicked the tin trash can parked outside the building's entrance. "Give me a break, Jack Cunningham really doesn't *remember* us? What, like he hit his head on a rock and got amnesia? Ridiculous!"

I grabbed Valentina's forearm gently and tugged her toward the quad. "Come on, V, let's go. We need a plan B."

"More like plan C." She shook her head, our feet clacking against the hot cement walkway. The sun had come out more since we went into class, and it was casting an unfittingly bright tone onto the area. "He's got to be faking, right? Like, to get us off his trail or something."

I sucked my bottom lip into my mouth. "I don't know. That's not Jack's thing. Now, his sister on the other hand, she's a master manipulator. She has to be, to get far in her family. But Jack?"

She sighed. "Yeah, he's not a very good liar."

"He doesn't need to be," I explained. "He's always gotten everything handed to him, everyone has always done what he wanted. I mean, that much is clear even to me after knowing him for less than a year."

She shook her head again, her temper cooling down as we walked. "No, you're right. You're right…" She whispered that last part, looking vacantly ahead.

Two polished, good-looking guys whistled at us as we walked by, and Valentina snapped to attention, throwing up her middle finger at them without a second thought. She barely looked their way as she did it, lowering the gesture as they passed and turning back to me, resuming our conversation. "So, what are we thinking here? Like, Jack really has been in some kind of accident?"

"He doesn't look like it."

She shrugged. "What else?"

"Well…"

"Well?"

"What if the Order did something to him?" I offered, not sure exactly *how* the Order could mess with someone's memory, but not ruling it out. Who knew what they were capable of?

"*Hmph.*" Her eyebrow lifted. "You know that sounds insane, right?"

I tilted my head toward her. "V, *sane* left the building the minute I moved to Newport. Hello, pirates? Hidden treasure? Murderous secret societies? A little sci-fi action wouldn't throw me off at this point."

Valentina chuckled, and I smiled. Her eyes widened at my fleeting expression of happiness. "Okay, that's the first time I've seen you smile, in...I don't know how long."

My smile fell, and the reminder of what I'd lost had my mind starting to drift to that dark place.

Valentina bumped me with her hip and brought me back to the present, the threads I was starting to pull snapping.

The two of us stopped walking when we passed a large bulletin board with various flyers and announcements. A couple people lingered in front, browsing, then walked away. "You're enjoying this, aren't you?" Valentina's accusing smile had the corners of my lips turning back up.

"What? No! I don't want this V. I'm just, you know, enjoying spending time with you."

"Uh-huh," she snickered. "You just love a challenge, don't you Fontaine?"

I bumped her back, my hip hitting her upper thigh with our height difference. "So do you!" My skin shivered as Valentina's hands grabbed tight around my shoulders, squeezing me close to her side. Her lips went to my ear, the same buzzing feeling from earlier filling up my body. "Well we certainly do have a challenge on our hands, don't we?" I turned into her and wrapped my arms around her waist, breathing her in. The bare skin of her back stuck to my arms. I felt goosebumps spread across her skin, and whether it was from my touch or the almost crisp weather, I wasn't sure. I reveled in the feeling of our connection until she pulled away.

"And I think I have an idea." V's long arm reached behind me. There was a tearing sound before a piece of paper was produced in front of me, a flyer with a Greek symbol and some writing indicating an event this evening. I recognized the name from the fraternity that was tagged in Jack's beer pong photo from this morning. Jack's new fraternity.

"A Phi Gamma party? At the frat Jack's rushing?"

"Tonight," Valentina said. "Probably part of the whole rush thing. You're going to need a new outfit."

FOUR

———◆—◆—◆———

Honking horns and sirens filled the night air. After spending so much time in small-town Rhode Island, the boisterous sounds of the city that once fell unnoticed into the background now felt prominent and annoying. Its familiar discord reminded me of things better left forgotten: the coffee runs Dom and I would take before coming back here to study, the highfalutin events my mother once forced me into, things like gallery shows or pretentious parties and dances. A transient memory of the debutante ball I'd bailed on a few years ago tugged at something deep down, my anger and frustration from that day making a more sensible pairing than me and the guy I'd been forced to take as my date.

I grabbed the windowsill and pulled down, shutting out the distractions. It was silent now, the walls of my room shielding me from anything that wasn't the rolled-up piece of paper hidden in the back of my drawer. I stuck my hand in and pulled it out, unraveling the old document to its full width. My eyes scanned the aged ink, scribbled in such a way that the words were barely legible. But I knew what they said. *Bill of sale. Rose Island. Cunningham.* And perhaps the most important clue of all: *Fontaine.*

I never really let it go, this idea that my family was the true owner of Rose Island, and all of Malloy's treasure, and that the Cunnighams had forced a sale behind their backs, doing what they do best. But I also wondered what the pirate Malloy was like. He'd only taken from the rich, in what I guessed was his way of attempting to break down the rich-poor gap at the time. If only he knew his plan would backfire, causing an even bigger group of privileged assholes to form an entire society to make sure that gap was never bridged and that the power would always stay in the hands of the man with the most money. It would crush him, just as it did me, to realize his efforts were for nothing.

But mine wouldn't be.

"Harper?" The door creaked open behind me, and instead of jamming the paper back in its hiding place, I felt my mind ballooning out, succumbing back to the wedding, hearing my name called over and over again. The screams were in my ears again and I dropped the paper, pressing my hands over my ears, willing the noise to quiet.

"Harper, are you okay?" Valentina rushed into the room, forcing my attention from the place it'd been. I hadn't even realized I'd covered my ears, and my hands shook as I let them fall. V's fingers looped loosely through mine as she closed the space between us, eyebrows furrowed in concern just like my mothers had been this morning. My eyes met hers accidentally, and an uncomfortable tingle zipped up my spine. I avoided her gaze, my focus shifting to the floor. *The paper.* Lodged between my feet and hers, the document had rolled back up into its usual posture. A crunching noise startled me as Valentina took another step toward me. I threw myself to the ground and ripped the paper from beneath her moving foot, screaming "Valentina, no!"

Valentina stumbled back, confused. "Harper, what?"

Harper. Harper. Harper.

"Stop!" I shouted, anger racing through my veins. Millions of tender nerves shot off throughout my body, begging to be calmed. "Stop calling my name!" I tightened my fist, accidentally crumpling the document even further.

"Goddamnit!" I cursed, releasing the paper slightly and turning to the drawer, placing it where it belonged. The sound of the drawer slamming punctuated my sentence, leaving Valentina and me in tense silence.

"Har—" Valentina started to address me again but stopped herself. "What the hell is going on?"

I breathed deeply, trying to shake the feelings I knew weren't Valentina's fault. I continued to face the drawer with my back to her, hands on the surface of the table and head drooped.

"I'm sorry," I whispered. "I didn't mean that." My heartbeat slowed, and so did the intense sensations throughout my body.

I heard something shift behind me, like maybe Valentina had reached out to touch me and stopped herself.

"I thought we were done with secrets," Valentina whispered back, hurt clinging to every word.

"We are," I choked out.

Valentina stepped up beside the desk, trying to get my attention. "Then what were you just hiding from me?"

I pressed my lips together and chanced a look at her. Valentina's dark hair was twisted into space buns, her eyeliner done to perfection. Her face seemed so different all done up, I had to blink a few times to get it together. "It just isn't...I didn't think it mattered anymore."

She sighed. "It doesn't look that way to me."

I closed my eyes and pressed my fingers to my lids. "After what happened, I just, I couldn't talk about it. Any of it. And what did it matter anyway, if the Order was going to get what they wanted?" I dropped my hands. "At first, I wanted to do something, *anything* to get revenge for Dom. But then Adan was put on house arrest, and it became clear if I did anything, it would only get worse for him. So I did nothing. I said nothing."

Another stretch of silence filled the space between us. "It's not just Adan either. Rebecca could—"

"Rebecca?"

My stomach dropped. Like I said, I hadn't really talked much about Dom's death. Which meant no one but me knew the role Rebecca played in it.

Valentina's hand went to her mouth. She clenched her jaw and took an angry breath, then turned away from me. "What does Rebecca Cunningham have to do with all this? I thought Allastair was the one who controlled the Order, not his granddaughter?"

I rubbed my toes on the carpet, trying to find the words to explain. "He does. But so does Rebecca, apparently. She has her own little games going. And right now, we're one of them. It was Rebecca who had Dom killed, not Allastair." My voice came out quieter, the next words difficult to say. "She was trying to keep Allastair from coming for me." I shrugged. "She wanted to get rid of me, since Allastair wanted me gone. But she did it her way." The phantom smell of chlorine seemed to sneak out of my mind and into the room for a moment. My voice shook. "This was her way of exercising control. On all of us. She's why Adan was arrested. But she's also why he got off."

Valentina threw her hands up into the air and started pacing. "I can't believe this, Harper. I can't understand why you wouldn't just tell me. Everything's always a secret with you. With us, there can *only* be secrets, right?"

I turned around and opened the drawer, grabbing the bill of sale and handing it to Valentina. "There's one more thing."

She opened it, her eyes widening as it scanned the messy writing.

"You know what this means, right?" I asked. Valentina lowered the paper and nodded slowly.

"Yeah...I do."

I put one hand over hers, crinkling the paper in her grasp a little as I tried to squeeze it. "This is what we need from Jack. He had his own search for Malloy's treasure going apart from his family. We know, we were a part of it. If he knows anything else important, like if Malloy had a will, something to prove the fortune is Fontaine money, or something to prove the sale was forced, we would have a shot at shifting the power. It's reasonable he wouldn't share that with us, being that I'm a Fontaine. We could stop the Order."

Valentina shook her head. "I wish you'd have told me why we were doing this all in the first place. I thought it was because of Dom, or my brother…because of whatever he's been holding back."

I raised my eyebrows. "Speaking of your brother, I'm not the only one keeping secrets."

She frowned. "My dad was too. And your grandfather. Everyone was. But we have to be more careful than them, Harper. We have to be different. It's the secrets that got them all killed. You have to tell me everything from now on." Her face softened. "Is that it?"

I nodded.

"Okay. I don't want to fight. We're on the same side here," she said softly. The girl in front of me was so different from the person I'd met in her kitchen the day I moved to Newport. The old V was willing to sabotage others at any opportunity, and always put herself first. How funny to imagine we ended up here, like this.

A forced smile appeared on V's face. "Now, let's get out of here. We have a party to go to, and your pants look like they're going to cut off your circulation. Might as well get this over with."

I grabbed my phone from the desk and shoved it in my pocket in agreement.

"Tell me where you got these again?" I asked, wishing Valentina would let me wear my own clothes.

"Nina," Valentina winked. "She may not be talking to you, but she still cares, Harper."

I breathed out. My girlfriend and I were about to crash our first college frat party. Nina would be a really good asset to have right now. Too bad she was in another state. But V and I *could* do this, right?

At that moment, I'd rather be wading into a freezing cold ocean or climbing through a vent. But no such luck. Phi Gamma, here we come.

FIVE

"You're super hot and everything, both of you, but forget it," a lazy sounding sophomore drawled as he blocked the front door to the Phi Gamma house. The place wasn't your typical movie-style mansion, but was instead a brownstone in the middle of the Upper West Side. Multiple fraternities and sororities were housed down this strip, making it easy to find.

"Um, I'm sorry, why not?" Valentina asked, crossing her arms and pivoting her hip, showing off her impeccable curves in her bodycon dress that left nothing to the imagination.

"You're that girl from Psych, right?"

I pinched my nose. *Shit, he was in that class.* I could see where this was going.

V's eyes narrowed. "So what?"

The guy raised his shoulders, his shaggy hair bouncing a little. "'*Drinking is stupid and even college kids shouldn't do that?*" He paraphrased Valentina's words from class. "Sounds familiar? Well, we like to drink here, so you should go play Barbies somewhere else."

I didn't blink. If I had, I'd have missed the warning signs—Valentina's shoulders lifting to her ears, her lips curling into an angry snarl—and I wouldn't have been able to catch her elbows before she mauled the guy. But I knew V, and I knew she'd go for his throat. So I grabbed her just in time, whispering my best attempts at calming her as I dragged her toward the stone steps and back onto the sidewalk. Well, I guess some things do stay the same.

"What the hell!" We both shouted at the same time as we landed a safe distance from the college kid.

"Why are *you* saying 'what the hell'?" I asked V, my hands in the air. "I should be saying it. You were gonna kill that guy!"

Valentina huffed and rolled her eyes. "We need to get inside, Harper, Jack is in there!" We knew because we'd passed Jack's bodyguards lingering inside a black van nearby. I almost didn't see them, considering how dark their windows were tinted, but the Newport license plate tipped me off.

This time, I rolled my eyes. "Duh, V, I know. But you weren't having any luck. You kind of screwed us with the drinking thing," She scoffed. "We need another way inside."

Valentina shook her head. "Okay, any ideas?"

I looked around, desperate for something to pop into my head. Picking a lock would be easier than crashing a college party at this point, something I never thought possible with Valentina Vasquez on my arm. I pressed my fingers to the metal chain on my neck that Valentina had given me as a gift once. The dips and curves entertained my anxious fingertips as I surveyed the area.

Something caught my eye. I cocked my head. "No way."

"What?" V asked, coming up next to me.

"No fucking way." I whispered this time, my brain trailing off to a time I'd tried to forget, to a world full of ball gowns, dancing, and endless rehearsals.

"What?" V asked a little more forcefully this time. "That brunette chick with the long wavy hair?" The girl stood in front of a similar brownstone across the street, bearing its own Greek letters indicating a sorority. She wore a pair of denim shorts and a T-shirt displaying the sorority name *Delta Phi*.

"Shalene," I explained. "I know her."

A strange look passed over Valentina's face. "Like, you dated?"

"Ew!" I crinkled my nose. "No!"

"What? She's pretty. She looks like Indian royalty or something. Like a princess." She wasn't wrong. Shalene's hair fell in luscious, dark waves around her angular face, her posture befitting someone who sat through finishing school as a kid without a single complaint.

I shot Valentina a look. "No, we know each other because...because our parents knew each other." I hesitated, my mind starting to pull on memories from that time, but I shook it off and cut Valentina a flirty look instead. "I don't need a princess when I have a queen."

Valentina smirked, then looked from the sorority house to the fraternity behind us. "You think she can get us in?"

I smiled. "Shalene's a few years older than us. She won't be rushing. In fact, she looks kind of important." Shalene stood on the sidewalk welcoming rushees, shaking their hands or hugging if the moment struck. She radiated the grace and charm my mother always wished I had in comparison.

"So, yes?" V asked, and I nodded.

"Let's go."

"Shalene!" I shouted, fake delight crossing my features as Valentina and I strode toward her. I wasn't very good at this kind of thing, but I had to try. Something about V and I being on a mission gave me a burst of energy I hadn't felt in months.

"Harper Fontaine?" A mix of young women sprinkled past us, greeting each other and stepping inside. Shalene and I did a little swerving until we finally stood in front of one another.

"So strange running into you," I offered, attempting to stick my hands in my pockets but realizing the fabric was too tight. Uncomfortable, I wriggled around a little bit until I felt Valentina's hand on my lower back. "Oh, and this is my girlfriend, Valentina."

Shalene's eyes flashed in surprise, then jumped to V. "Nice to meet you," she said with an endearing smile, her throaty voice sounding out of place with her valley girl accent. "Harper, I didn't know you were back in New York."

I shrugged. Duh, of course she didn't. I wasn't exactly announcing my return or diving back into the social scene. Until now, apparently. "Um, yeah," I said, not wanting to elaborate.

"So what are you doing here? That was a quick stint in Rhode Island. I mean, I know you weren't pregnant." Shalene winked at Valentina and leaned in a little closer to me. "Rehab?" Valentina snorted.

"No," I forced a laugh, trying to sound casual. "Nothing like that. Just spending a year with my dad, that's all. We're actually here to get into that party." I jutted my thumb behind me, pointing at the metaphorical tower Jack was locked in at this very moment.

Shalene placed her hands on her hips. "Ooh, a Phi Gamma party, huh." She cocked her head. "Never thought I'd see the day."

I bit my lip. "Yeah, we know someone in there from Newport, we're just trying to connect with him. We tried getting into the party but we...ran into some trouble. Is there any chance..." I paused, wondering if Shalene would take the hint and offer to help us.

"Can you get us in?" V cut in, her impatience showing.

Shalene's fingers wrapped around her chin in curiosity. "I see." She paused, her eyes assessing me. "Intriguing. Come with me." I almost spun around on my heel in the direction of the fraternity but stopped when I noticed her gliding up the stone staircase into her sorority house. Valentina grabbed my arm and shot me a confused look, and I just shook my head, as if to say *I have no idea what's happening either.*

The gliding continued until Shalene made it up three flights of stairs to her bedroom, which I imagined was one of the biggest rooms in the building, considering its size. The room itself was classic Manhattan, with small windows and brick walls that brought an urban charm to the probably ancient space. It was hard to notice the structure of the room, however, when the decor gave you so much to look at.

The space was colorful, with a vibrant patterned bedspread as the centerpiece, its rich teal and gathered floral design matching the throw pillows tossed neatly onto a nearby chair. A plush floor rug the color of a deep purple tied the room together. Instead of paper posters, the walls showcased framed artwork, a mix of flowers and shapes staring back at us.

Shalene took a seat at a vanity, clicking on the lightbulbs surrounding the mirror frame. Multiple jewelry boxes sat organized on the desk's surface, and the entire space had a pristine feel that made me wonder if Shalene had hired a maid.

Valentina and I stood awkwardly in the center of the room as Shalene pulled open one of her drawers and produced a makeup brush and some translucent powder. She popped open the compact and dabbed the brush inside, then lifted the brush to her face. As she did, our eyes met in the mirror, and Shalene let them linger momentarily.

"So Harper," she began, finally releasing my gaze and lowering the brush onto her skin. "Getting into this party seems important to you. Am I wrong?" The soft pink bristles grazed the powder once more, then dabbed gently on Shalene's skin as she kept her focus on the mirror. "I mean, it must be, otherwise you wouldn't be asking me for a favor."

My mouth went dry, and I licked my lips. Where was she going with this? "Um, well yeah, sure. I'd really like to get into that party."

"Mhm," Shalene acknowledged, closing her compact and letting it rest in her hands. "Right. Do you remember my sister, Shyla? She's a little younger than you?" Shyla was a much worse version of Shalene. Everyone called her "Little S", something that was probably started by Shalene herself in an attempt to mold her sister in her image, but instead created a monster. Even I could tell Shyla hated living in her sister's shadow. Still, Shalene assumed the dedicated role of big sister, doing everything in her power to look out for her in whatever way she saw fit.

"Um, yeah," I said, glancing once again in Valentina's direction, silently praying for some kind of save I knew she couldn't offer.

Shalene wheeled around in her chair and faced me. "You might be interested to know that it's her debutante year. My mother is part of the committee again, just as she was during our year." My stomach plummeted at the mention of the debutante ball.

Valentina scoffed. "*Our year?* Harper, you were a deb?" I cringed, shame crawling up my spine. I'd hoped we'd make it through this conversation without bringing any of this up.

"She sure was," Shalene confirmed, her voice lilting in such a way that made me nervous. "In fact, Harper's introduction was just before mine. And when she didn't show up, that took all the steam away from my entrance."

I shrunk back, sheepish. "Oh come on Shalene, no one even noticed I wasn't there."

"Jeremy noticed," Shalene protested, standing up and crossing her arms. "Her date," she clarified for Valentina, eyes jumping between us.

"Was that his name?" I said guiltily, my voice quiet.

Shalene threw her hair over her shoulder. "Poor guy, when you didn't show he stood there all by himself. Not to mention he had to sit out on the deb dance since he didn't have a partner. The whole performance was messed up. My mother was so embarrassed. Everyone thought she'd organized a terrible event."

"Look, this is really interesting and all, but if I wanted the Cliff Notes on Harper's past I'd read her diary. What does all this have to do with the party?" Valentina took a step closer to me. I wanted to throw my arms around her and thank her.

"Glad you asked!" Shalene's voice pitched up, a fake smile pinned to her cheeks. "See, here's the thing Harper. You want something, I want something. My mother is organizing the debutante ball again this year, and it's her chance to reclaim her reputation. It's also an opportunity for my sister's year to be noticed. It should be a night no one forgets. I refuse to let what happened to me happen to her. And that's why I want *you* to come out this year."

My chest seized with panic, and even though Shalene's meaning clicked immediately, I said, "It's a little late for that." My left hand raised and waved towards Valentina. "I came out years ago. Hence the girlfriend." V laughed, amused at my joke, but Shalene's smile pressed into a line.

"Harper, it might not make sense to you, considering you *ruined* our ball, but you actually have some notoriety around here. Going back to Newport reminded a lot of people where you come from. You're one of the Six Families, a *Fontaine*. That means something, even around here. If you show up, attend all the rehearsals and meetings, do everything you're supposed to do, including *show up*," she repeated, "you will make everyone look good."

I thought I'd left all that crap in Rhode Island— the froofy dresses and high society expectations, pretending to be someone I'm not. That should all be behind me now. I was in New York for Christ's sake. People could be whatever they wanted here. I was no one. At least, I thought I was.

"It was a choice," Shalene said.

"Huh?"

"Leaving Jeremy to present himself alone was a choice. Ditching the debutante ball was a choice." *Just like being invisible here in New York was a choice.* "Now, you have another chance. How much do you want to get into this party?"

I snuck a glance at Valentina, whose eyes were wide with questions. How far was I willing to go? I hesitated, wondering if there was another way to get Jack alone again—away from the prying eyes of his bodyguards—without making this deal.

"Look," Shalene added, her arms still crossed. It was Shalene against us, but we stood in an almost triangle-like formation in her room, just a couple years too old for a pillow fight or game of truth or dare. But this wasn't a sleepover, and we weren't playing. This was blackmail. "It's against Greek policy, and the school's, to pretend you're in my sorority when you're not. Not to mention you're underage and there will be drinking there. I could get in serious trouble. But like it or not, that's the only way I can get you into the frat parties you're looking for. The Phi Gamma house isn't stupid enough to let in non-college kids, and right now, parties are for rushees only. This is your shot. As the president of Delta Phi, I'd be risking a lot to get you guys into the fraternity. So either you take my request to participate in the debutante ball this season and you get into that party, or don't, and you go home."

I could see Valentina nodding beside me, attempting to catch my eye and encourage me to take the offer. I closed my eyes, the heaviness of the commitment I was about to make weighing on me.

"If I do this, it's not just this one party. If there are other parties we need to get into, or like, info we need on certain people at Columbia, or whatever, you've got to be our source."

One corner of Shalene's mouth ticked up. "Done. Come with me, ladies, the party is just getting started. And Harper?" she said. "Good luck."

SIX

---◆◆◆---

"Please tell me we're not just going to stand here looking stupid," Valentina asked as we lingered behind the doorway to the living room. Despite being a city building, the first floor was pretty big, and we could see Jack inside from where we were standing at the kitchen threshold.

"No, of course not," I whispered, which was probably a little too quiet considering how loud the party was. Music boomed from somewhere, and shiny red solo cups littered every surface. I glanced to our left, an empty hallway diverging from the two rooms. My attention moved back to Jack, who was now moving. "Come on, come on," I mumbled to myself, and V took a tiny step behind me to avoid being seen. "We just need to get him where we want him."

"Which would be…?" Valentina said into my hair, her hand going to my arm as Jack moved toward us, a little shaky on his feet, amber liquid spilling from his plastic cup. I took a step back into Valentina, and she let me crush her up against the wall as we half-hid behind the doorway. Jack thankfully was too inebriated to let his gaze land directly on us.

"Right here," I whispered behind me, my arms reaching out and pushing Jack down the open hallway, his feet stumbling as he tripped over himself. It was easy, guiding Jack, because the poor guy didn't realize what was happening.

"Hey," he slurred, arms catching on the wall as Valentina and I cornered him. I glanced over my shoulder, but people passed by without giving us a second look. "This isn't the bathroom."

"We'll take you to the bathroom when we've finished talking," I demanded.

"It's you guys," Jack said. "The weird girls."

Valentina rolled her eyes. "Listen up Jack, we're not playing around. Do you know who these people are?" V pulled out her phone with her right hand, her left hand pressed up against Jack's shoulder, pinning him to the wall. On her screen was a photo of her dad, Adan Vasquez Sr., and my grandfather, Nathaniel.

He squinted. "No, that one kind of looks like you though," Jack said, sticking a finger at Mr. Vasquez.

Valentina looked over at me. "Jack should know my dad," she said.

"Oh, he is your dad? Cool," Jack giggled, a little snort following shortly behind. Valentina closed her eyes in frustration.

"He's too drunk. We didn't think this through."

"Wait," he said, grabbing Valentina's phone from her hand. "Is that the lighthouse by my house?" *House* was a generous word. Mansion was more like it.

My heartrate picked up speed. "Yes! Yes Jack, it is. Do you remember what it's called?"

He shrugged, handing the phone back to V. "No, why would I? I've never been there."

All hope I'd had plummeted. "Well, hold on," he added, leaning into the photo in her hands and squinting. "Maybe I have been there." He tapped a finger to his chin and looked up. "No, I guess not."

"Yes, you have been there." Valentina corrected forcefully. "That's Rose Island, remember? You could get into it from an underground bunker connected to the Castle Hill Lighthouse."

Jack cocked his head. "Never been there either."

"Ah!" Valentina made a guttural sound. "This is ridiculous!"

"Shh," I held up a hand to V. "Just, give him a minute."

"I mean, maybe I went there on a field trip or something?" he offered, scratching his head. His pupils were dilated, which could mean a lot of different things, but I couldn't help but notice the far off look in his eye. He was focusing, trying to remember. Rose Island must be sitting in the back of his mind, itching to rise to the surface. Maybe if he pulled at the strings for long enough, it would.

"No Jack, it was the Order. The Order of the Six. Think about that for a second. *There Can Only Be Six*, remember?" I repeated his catch phrase from the induction ceremony and the trials he'd put us through last winter, then relaxed my right hand, which was pressed to his right shoulder, securing him in place. He didn't try to leave, just stood there and tossed that information around in his brain.

"The crest!" I remembered. "V, where was his tattoo?" I asked.

Her eyes widened and she considered my question. "His shoulder blade. That one, I think." She pointed to the side I'd just been holding.

I shrugged. "We have to show him. He might not believe us if we don't."

Valentina hesitated, then glanced at me.

I shrugged. "Do it. The importance that he remember the Order far outshines our need to respect his personal space at this minute."

She nodded back at me, then grabbed the collar of Jack's shirt and pulled outwards hard, the first four buttons popping instantaneously. She pulled again until half his shirt was open, and Jack let out a little, "Hey!" until he realized what she was doing. Or at least, until he realized what he *thought* she was doing. His pupils snapped back to their normal size, this false world he lived in becoming his reality once more. "Should we look for a room?" Jack asked, leaning in toward Valentina, lips pursed.

"Ew!" She spat, her palm pressing against his face, pushing him away. I chuckled, not being able to help myself. Had Jack been so *not* V's type, I might have been jealous, but the idea of Jack Cunningham trying to kiss Valentina Vasquez was so ridiculous that I had to laugh.

"Oh be quiet," she whispered to me, and, with renewed determination, the two of us yanked his shirt off his shoulder, revealing bare skin. Jack stumbled a little, but he let us continue as we checked the other shoulder too. No tattoo there, either.

"Wait," V said, switching back to the first side and shining her phone's flashlight on it. "I was sure it was here."

And it was. It *was* there. Meaning, past tense. With the fluorescent light shining on Jack's pale skin, the slight trace of the crest of the Order of the Six peered through to us.

"It's gone," Valentina breathed. "They removed it."

Jack rolled his eyes, probably thinking we were nuts. "You girls are crazy, you know that?" But when he glanced down at his shoulder blade, which V and I were still pulling forward enough that even he could see, his face fell. Despite the darkness of the shadowy hallway, I could see Jack's pupils grow in size once more.

"I…I never had a tattoo there."

"Yes, you did." V said.

Cunningham shook us off and grabbed the shoulder himself, as if he could pull it off his body and examine it.

"No I didn't. I've never had a tattoo." His voice pitched. "What are those lines? Is that a rose?" He squinted, confusion blossoming across his face. "This isn't right. I didn't have a tattoo, and I've never been to the stupid lighthouses in Newport. This is…this is…it doesn't make sense."

My attention was trained so hard on Jack that I almost screamed when Valentina yanked me into the nearby bathroom, leaving Jack behind.

"Hello, earth to Harper! Check your 6 o'clock!" Before Valentina closed the bathroom door, shutting us in, I spotted the two bodyguards heading this way through the threshold opening. When we were safely behind closed doors, neither of us said a word, pressing our ears up against the hollow doorway.

"There he is," one voice said. "Mr. Cunningham, sir, we're just checking in on you. We haven't heard from you in a while."

There was a pause, and then Jack's easy voice echoed back at us, as if the entire exchange we just had two seconds ago had never happened in the first place. "I told you fools not to come in here. It's an embarrassment. This is rush week, I basically won't be leaving this house until it's over."

"Certainly, Mr. Cunningham, we understand, it's just, we're under strict orders to—"

"That's enough. I plan to celebrate the first few weeks of school. If you have a problem with that, I'll be calling my grandfather and demanding he hire a different service. Don't forget who is in charge here."

One of the men cleared their throat. I wanted to laugh. Poor Jack, he was completely unaware that Dumb and Dumber here were not hired *for* Jack, but to keep tabs *on* him. Still, they probably didn't want to tip off their mark, so when footsteps began echoing down the hall, I assumed the men had agreed to back off a little, if not only temporarily.

We waited a moment, then opened the door. The coast was clear. *Too clear.* Jack was gone.

"His goons may be gone for now, but I think we've played our hand for the night," I said. "You saw Jack's face at the end there, he was remembering something. Maybe not totally, but he has access to it somewhere deep down. Getting him alone and forcing him to confront Order stuff might rattle him enough to remember."

Valentina stared emptily into the hallway. "We have to go hard, though. The Order did a number on him. Just showing him a few pictures isn't going to do it."

"I agree."

"Okay great, then we have a plan," V said.

I lifted my brow. "What do you mean?"

"I mean, we're going to kidnap Jack. And we're going to need Nina to do it."

SEVEN

———◆—◆—◆———

I looked down at my sneakers, the silence in the room deafening, until someone broke the tension.

"Um, you didn't like, kill him, did you?" Nina chirped, nodding at Jack who was passed out in an office chair that I'd taken the wheels off of before securing him tightly on it with thick rope. His head leaned off to the side on his shoulder, eyes bouncing around under his eyelids as if he was dreaming.

"Of course not!" I said, exasperated. "We waited until he passed out to drag him out here. He's alive." I bit my lip. I certainly didn't *want* to drag anyone anywhere. Especially not a drunk person. But there was no way to lure Jack out here without a little assistance from us, at least not without his guards noticing. Getting him alone was our only chance. Now that we knew what the Order was capable of, the stakes were just too high. And the truth was, I probably wouldn't have agreed to this at all if I didn't think Jack would thank us for it once we found some way to jog his memory. *If* we can jog his memory, that is.

"Here being...where, exactly?" I noticed Nina didn't look me in the eye when she spoke to me. So, she was still mad at me for what happened to Dom. I didn't blame her.

Valentina took a step forward, arms crossed as she watched Jack sleep. "This apartment building is undergoing renovation. It's paused at the moment, so no one should find us here. The best part? It's down the street from the frat house, so Harper and I were able to get him here without anyone noticing."

"Not that it was easy," I mumbled, thinking of the Uber driver who kept looking at V and I curiously as we hauled an unconscious Jack in and out of the car.

"And you just happened to find this place last night?" Nina questioned, skeptical.

I huffed out a breath. "Apparently V was hatching this plan before we even showed up at Jack's fraternity. No more secrets, right V?"

"Oh come on," she reasoned. "Did you really think we'd get what we needed from a quick chat in the middle of an empty hallway? These are *Cunninghams* we're dealing with. They don't do anything halfway."

"I can't believe you guys didn't invite me," Nina muttered, looking off to the side. Her brown curls were worn loose, probably unkempt due to her last-minute trip out here.

I took a step toward her and put my hand on her shoulder. We were lucky she was up for ditching school while her parents were away all week for her great grandmother's funeral. It wasn't like Nina to sacrifice her education, but then again she wasn't one to miss out, either. "Yes we did, Nina, that's why you're here."

"Yeah, to be some, like, extra guard to watch him while you guys run around the city!" She shrugged me off, and the action stung. "How long are we keeping him anyway?"

V nodded at Jack. "As long as it takes."

I rolled my eyes. "No, V, only for 24 hours, max. That's the most we can get away with before his security detail gets suspicious. And Nina, you're not just an extra set of eyes. We need to question him when he wakes up. He doesn't remember the Order. We're trying to remind him of that and find out what he knows. You both grew up with him, so you know him best."

She pursed her lips, the plan becoming more appealing. "Okay, so who is going to play bad cop?"

V and I both let out a chuckle. If anyone in this room was going to play bad cop, I wouldn't expect it to be Nina. She turned to me, her face serious.

"Hey, I haven't totally forgiven you yet. You should be on my side."

I closed my eyes, took a deep breath, then opened them. "Nina, haven't I been punished enough? I lost my best friend." Her face fell. A grunt spilled from Jack's lips as he stirred a few feet away, his eyes still closed.

"Okay fine," Nina whispered to me, taking a step closer. "You can be the good cop. But let me take the lead." She spun on her heel and prodded Jack in the shoulder, rousing him.

"Okay Jack, it's time to spill everything you know!" Nina shouted, her tiny voice sounding strange as it bounced off the walls of the empty room.

Jack blinked a few times, then looked down at his body, acknowledging the rope. Each of his arms were tied to the armrests of the chair. He balled his fists, attempting to yank himself off the chair. Nothing budged. He struggled again, then stalled. "I won't tell you anything."

Nina swaggered toward Jack until she was right in front of him. Valentina and I locked eyes, then rolled them simultaneously. "Oh, I think you will," Nina said.

Jack snorted and looked Nina up and down. "Judging by your shoes and the baby fat on your cheeks, I'd say you go to my old high school with those two." His chin jutted towards me and V. Nina's cheeks reddened, and I couldn't help but laugh. She shot me a look.

"And you," Jack said, pointing his scrutiny toward me. "I'm not sure what to do with you. You look like you pretend you're not rich, but you still manage to get your hair deep conditioned every month."

It was my turn to go red. "I do not!"

He chortles. "You use expensive products at the very least."

"Don't worry Harper, I'll handle this," Nina said, as she slapped Jack clean across the face. "Tell us everything!" I winced, about to intervene, but Jack spoke.

"Never!" he protested. Nina slapped him again, this time in the other direction.

"Start talking Cunningham!"

Jack wriggled around in his chair again. "You can hit me all you want; I'll never reveal any secrets."

I pulled Nina away from Jack and muttered under my breath, "I said *question* Jack, not *interrogate* him."

"Ooh, nice good cop," she winked, and I pressed my hands to my head in exasperation.

"Hey!" Jack yelled. Nina and I turned to see Valentina, pulling his tie off his neck and dangling it in front of him.

"The cost of this tie would make any grown man cry." V pulled out a pair of nail scissors from her purse and held them up to the fabric. "If it's ruined, I mean."

"No, no please, it's vintage! I'll tell you!"

Nina rushed to Valentina's side. "You said I could be bad cop!"

V shrugged, still holding the expensive accessory in her hands. "It wasn't working. Let's play to our strengths, shall we?"

"Release the tie," Jack pleaded. "Listen, I don't know why you girls are even on my case. I'm new to Phi Gamma. Is this because I was exempt from hazing? It's not my fault I'm important." The tone in his voice went from desperate to haughty, and my patience grew thin. "If you're trying to take them down, there's plenty of proof of the hazing. They film everything on their phones. If you just get your hands on one, you have everything you need. Just leave me out of it."

Nina's face scrunched up. "That's not what we're asking about, Jack. The *Order*, hello!"

This time, Jack rolled his eyes. "Not this again. I thought we were finished playing games."

I waved Nina and V over to me and led us out into the hallway, closing the door behind us.

"He doesn't remember, Nina."

"What? Then why were we questioning him?" She asked, baffled.

I shrugged. "We wanted you to see for yourself. It's kind of hard to explain."

Nina looked from me to Valentina. "So, you weren't kidding about all that stuff on the phone then. I thought you were exaggerating to get me out here." Valentina shook her head solemnly. "So, what, he's brainwashed?"

"We think so," I said.

Nina bit her lip. "Then what's the plan? You must have one if you kidnapped him."

"Temporarily detained," I corrected, hoping those words sounded less like the felony this definitely was.

"There was one thing that seemed to help him remember," Valentina interjected. "When he was drinking, his inhibitions were loosened, his mind was open."

I nodded. "He was a lot easier to manipulate."

"So we get him drunk?" Nina asked, not sure which of us to ask.

Valentina looked at me, encouraging me to say it. "Actually, we had a different thought. But we need Jack on board for this."

Nina snorted. "This ought to be good."

A few minutes later the three of us stood in a line in front of Jack, our arms crossed. We looked like Charlie's Angels, what with our varying heights and hair colors. It did nothing to intimidate Jack, however, which I guess wasn't a surprise for someone who grew up with Rebecca Cunningham as an older sister.

"I'm sorry, can you repeat that?" he asked, his vision making its way down the line. "I must have misheard you, because what you just said was too ridiculous to be true."

"Sure," I said, taking a deep breath. "We want to hypnotize you."

The corner of his mouth turned down on one side. "Oh, you're serious."

"Yes, we're serious. Don't you want to remember who you are? Where you came from?" I asked, and Jack snapped.

"I *do* know who I am. And I know where I came from! You girls are Looney Tunes. Nothing you can do will make me agree to have my mind meddled with by some quack."

Valentina leaned into me. "He has to be willing in order for it to work."

"Then we make him willing," I whispered back.

"Do we get the vodka now?" Nina asked, leaning into me from the other side.

"No," I answered. "There was one thing that seemed to really get to Jack. We have one move left." *Jack's tattoo,* I thought. Jack was shaken when we saw the empty spot on his shoulder. It was as if somewhere deep in his brain he knew something was supposed to be there. Lucky for us, we had the missing piece. I pulled the sleeve up on my right arm and shoved my skin in his face. The symbol of the Order of the Six stood out in black ink against my pale flesh, a delicate rose poised on the north end of a compass. Jack's eyes bugged out, and I noticed his arms move, like he was trying to reach for my arm through the rope.

"That...I've seen that before," he whispered. "What is that?"

"You know what it is, Cunningham. You just don't remember," Valentina said.

"It's the crest of the Order of the Six," I explained. "You had one too, right there." I pulled his shirt back over his shoulder. Jack paused before looking at it, but when he did, he began to sweat. A vein on the side of his neck jumped wildly, his blood pumping through his body. If you looked closely, you could see the marks where the tattoo had once been. It was undeniable proof we were telling the truth.

Whatever the Order had done to brainwash Jack, it had to have taken months. And it was done well, too. But it wasn't foolproof. There had to be a back door, or a way to crack the hold this had on him. What if Allastair had hoped Jack would come around one day? He'd need to be able to undo what they'd done. Or maybe their technology wasn't as good as they thought it was. Either way, Jack couldn't deny something had happened to him. There was so much he didn't know. If we could convince him to agree to a hypnotism, maybe we could unlock those memories that were clearly lingering somewhere out of touch.

"Oh," Nina reached into her pocket and pulled out her phone. "And how about this?" she asked, pulling up a photo and shoving it in Jack's face. I didn't think his eyes could widen any more than they already had, but somehow, they did.

"That's photoshopped." He darted his eyes around the room, unsure where to settle his gaze. "It's got to be."

"It's not," she corrected, swiveling the phone to me and Valentina. Nina and Jamie, the only other member in our Order chapter besides us and Adan, sat on a leather sofa and smiled widely at the camera. The photo had been taken in the Castle Hill bunker. Standing behind them and holding a piece of paper was Jack, his feet pressed squarely into the corner of the Order's crest that was inked into the floor. You couldn't see the whole thing, but it was clear what it was. She turned it to Jack again, and a flash of something crossed his face. It wasn't recognition, but *almost.*

Jack shook his head. "You're lying," he said, but the shake in his voice told me he wasn't convinced of that.

"Now I understand the bodyguards," Valentina said to me and Nina, but I could tell Jack was listening too. "They're not just so Jack doesn't run into other Order members like us, but so he doesn't interact with *anything* related to the Order that might trigger a memory."

"That's pish posh. Damien and Nick are for my protection."

Nina threw her head back and laughed. "Oh please, as if you're *famous*."

Valentina flipped her hair. "Has anyone besides us recognized you since you got here?" Jack's face relaxed as he considered this. "Has anyone…asked you for your autograph?" she added. "No?"

Jack's face fell. The little reality check had seemed to extinguish some of his panic, bringing him down to earth.

"Think about it," I continued for V. "Why would a bunch of high schoolers from your hometown come here to ask you about fraternity secrets?" I got on one knee in front of him and put my hand on his arm. "Your grandfather did this to you. He took away your memory of a very important secret society you used to be a part of. You used to be a *leader*." His eyes flashed at that. "You were way more important than a random college frat boy. He took that from you. We are trying to get the truth. That's all we want. And you," I lifted my tattooed arm to his gaze once again, "want it too. I can tell."

Jack was quiet.

Valentina grabbed her phone from her purse and opened up her photo album, scrolling back a couple years. When she landed on a cluster of photos from middle school, she stopped.

"If we don't know you, why do I have pictures of us together from the 8th grade cruise? Or how about pics from your family's annual Christmas party?" Her fingers moved as she scrolled by each photo. Jack's face was tight, and the silence was all the admission I needed. He knew something was wrong, and with the evidence in his face, he couldn't deny it.

"What's the worst that can happen? If you agree, you have a chance to learn the truth. To confirm your grandfather did what we said he did. Or," I stood up. "You can go back to your little frat house and wonder every day for the rest of your life why two burly dudes are following you everywhere."

Jack frowned, but his eyes shone intently. "Fine. I'll do it." He looked across the row of us. "But only if one of you agrees to be hypnotized as well."

EIGHT

Nina rolled her eyes. "Come on! This is so unfair! Why do I have to be the most mentally stable person in the room?"

Valentina shrugged. "Well, you have two parents that love you."

"And apart from being one of the Six wealthiest families in New England, you've had a pretty normal life," I added, peeking over my shoulder at Jack. His lips were pursed nonchalantly, but I could tell he was trying to listen in as Nina, Valentina and I huddled in the corner. The empty space in the room bounced our voices around, which wasn't helping to keep our conversation private.

"I knew that was going to come back to bite me one day!" Nina complained. V put her hand on Nina's arm.

"Trust me, it's a good thing."

Jack snorted. "Who would ever want to be ordinary?"

Nina looked like she was going to say something, so I stepped in front of her, blocking Jack from her view. I shook my head, as if to say *just ignore him,* and she did.

"Fine, I'll do it. But Jack has to be hypnotized first. Like hell I'm doing this only so he can back out at the last minute. Where is this psychologist or…psychotherapist, or…psych-whatever you found anyway, Valentina?"

Just then, there was a knock on the door. All of our heads turned in its direction. My heart sped up. It was interesting that Jack didn't immediately call out for help. Either he knew who was at the door, or he wanted answers more than he cared to admit. I didn't blame him; I'd want answers too.

"That's got to be Tiana." Valentina glided to the closed wooden door and opened it. An elegant woman about ten years older than us stepped into the room. A pang of familiarity hit me as I took in her dark skin and high cheekbones. Tiana's long braids were twisted into a neat bun on her head.

I leaned into Nina. "Um, is it just me, or does she look like—?"

"Sierra?" Valentina's ex-girlfriend stepped into the room next to Tiana, looking like a mini-me of the older woman. Though her presence was a complete surprise, it was the fact that Jack had just said her name that had me stunned into confused silence.

"He remembers *Sierra*?" Nina squealed, annoyed.

"Of course I remember Sierra," Jack said, glaring at Nina. "We went to Wellsley together."

I glanced from Sierra to Jack. "Well, Sierra wasn't associated with the Order. They'd have no reason to erase her from his mind. Kind of makes sense I guess." Nina nodded begrudgingly.

"And how do you all know each other?" Jack asked, his attention jumping around the room. There was a beat of silence. "I see," he added, and I bit down on my jaw.

"Valentina and I dated," Sierra interjected, her warm, friendly voice bringing a soothing tone to the tense space. "Briefly," she added, cutting an apologetic gaze towards me. I waved her off. Sierra and Valentina dated a long time ago. I hadn't even been in Newport when they were a thing. I mean, unless you count their "close friendship" from this summer. Valentina swore up and down that Sierra was just a good friend to her during all the drama with her mom and my dad's wedding, but it had looked like more than that. And considering she'd just showed up to help us engage in criminal activity, I had to wonder.

"Okay," Jack said. He jutted his chin in Tiana's direction. "Are you qualified?"

Tiana wandered deeper into the room. "Well, that depends on what you're looking for. I was asked to perform a hypnotism. If that's what you're wondering, then yes, I'm qualified."

Sierra took a step forward, her pleasant smile a little out of place for the current situation. "I'm sorry, I didn't mean to be rude. This is my cousin Tiana. She's been studying psychotherapy since I was in middle school. She can do what you're looking for."

"I can. But I do have to ask about…" Tiana's gaze flicked to Jack's restraints, and I blushed.

"Oh, uh, don't worry about that. Jack is a totally willing participant." I rushed over to Jack's chair and loosened the ties on his wrists, bending down on one knee. "Don't get any ideas Jack, we're doing this," I muttered so only he could hear. Jack made eye contact with me as he yanked his hands from the chair's grasp, then rubbed them tenderly. I left his ankles tied, however, just in case.

"I'll need assurances that this session will be completely confidential. My family is incredibly powerful," Jack said, his eyes scanning the room. *If you only knew,* I thought.

Sierra placed a hand on Jack's shoulder. "Don't worry Jack, whatever happens in this room, stays in this room. Confidentiality is one of the first things they teach you in the mental health field. Tiana couldn't practice without it." His face softened, and part of me was suddenly grateful for the presence of a familiar face. Maybe Sierra and her connection to Jack would bring Jack much needed reassurance.

After a moment, Jack nodded at Tiana.

"Okay then. Can we get some chairs? Let's get comfortable."

As Nina helped Tiana and Sierra arrange the seating we'd gathered from other offices in the building, I stood in the back of the room with Valentina, observing, our voices quiet below the hushed chatter of the group and squeak of the moving chairs. "I don't want to sound like, critical of Sierra or anything, she seems really nice, but how do we know we can trust her and Tiana? If this works, Jack is going to spill a lot of Order secrets. This is big stuff. How can you be sure they won't tell anyone?"

Valentina kept her eyes on the bustle in front of us. "Sierra and I grew up together. She's not like that. Her family does well enough, but she never fell quite in that 'one percent' group that she'd have needed to be recruited by the Order. I mean maybe she heard whispers about it, I don't know, but money and power, that stuff just isn't important to her." I hummed in acknowledgment. "And Tiana, well, the Vasquezs will be paying off her grad school loans."

I whistled. "That's got to be a lot of money."

Valentina nodded. "Sierra assured me that will be enough. And if it's not, we'll get to it when we get to it. This is the only chance we have."

The streetlights poured in behind the closed blinds of the windows. It had started getting dark in the time it had taken for V to get Tiana and Sierra over here. They were local, which was news to me, but at least that meant we could get things moving quickly.

"If we're ready?" Tiana asked, looking back at us and gesturing to the empty seats beside her. I let out a breath and nodded. Valentina took my hand and guided us to the metal chairs, where we sat in total silence.

"There is no need to be nervous," Tiana said, her voice firm and reassuring.

"I'm not," Jack scoffed, but the whites of his eyes told a different story.

"This is a metronome." Tiana pulled something out of her bag that was small and black. It looked like a 3-D triangle. She tapped the silver metal rod that was sticking up straight in the middle and it began bouncing back and forth, producing a rhythmic pulsing sound. It was the only noise in the room apart from our breathing and Tiana's voice.

"This will help you enter the hypnotic trance. Now Jack, focus on it, and try to relax. When you begin to drift off, you may close your eyes."

Jack shifted a little in his seat, allowing his palms to rest in his lap. His shoulders slumped against the chair and he leaned his head back, his eyesight pointed slightly downward as he followed directions and stared at the metronome.

"Breathe in," she directed. "And out." Jack did as he was told, repeating this step over and over until Tiana directed him to acknowledge and relax various parts of his body. As the rest of us watched, we could see Jack sinking deeper into his seat, his limbs resting heavily as Tiana worked her magic and lulled Jack into a deep state of hypnosis.

"Jack, I am going to count down to one, and with each number you will become more and more relaxed. Your mind will be at ease, and you may let go of whatever influence is blocking your subconscious. When I reach one, you will be in a trance, and your memories will be released." There was a beat of silence.

"Three." Tiana paused.

"Two." Another beat. Tiana looked over at us. Nina wrung her hands in her lap, her lips tight. Valentina's fingers gripped the edges of her chair, despite her every attempt to look relaxed. Even Sierra was sitting ramrod straight. But it was me whose nails dug into my knees, because I had the most to lose if this didn't work.

And it had better.

"*One.*" Jack's eyes popped open, his throat tensing with stalled effort as he sucked in an impossibly deep breath. Everyone froze, watching Jack's unfocused gaze as his eyes landed on a spot above our heads, open but unseeing. Or maybe he was seeing, but whatever it was, it wasn't in this room. It was deadly quiet, and eventually I realized Jack had not woken up from his trance. His eyes may have opened but he was sitting very still, his pupils dilated and unmoving as he stared off into space. I caught Tiana's eye to ensure this was normal, and she nodded.

"Jack, if you are with me, tap twice with your finger." There was a brief hesitation before Jack lifted his pointer finger and dropped it, then repeated the gesture. The sight was eerie, as if we were talking to a

comatose patient. Tiana continued. "Your mind is
open. The answers you seek live there, deep in your
subconscious. A small thing may trigger a memory, for
thoughts we once thought were lost to us are never
truly forgotten. Let the memories come back to you.
Whatever was done to you to refuse access, has floated
away." Tiana breathed in and closed her eyes, tapping
into something inside herself.

"If presently there remains any part of your
consciousness that is aware, switch it off. I am speaking
directly to your subconscious now."

Jack didn't move. Neither did Tiana. Instead, she
spoke softly. *"Remember what you have lost."* She paused.
"Remember." She paused again, then opened her eyes.
"Remember." Jack did not stir, causing Tiana to glance at
Sierra. Sierra nodded, encouraging her cousin to
continue.

"Remember…the Order of the Six."

Tiana's finger stilled the bouncing metronome,
stifling the room with silence. At her words, something
changed in Jack's eyes. I leaned forward, trying to
determine if I was seeing things, but no, I hadn't been.
Jack's pupils were morphing in size, larger to smaller,

then larger again. The hairs on my arms stood on end as a guttural noise began in Jack's throat, quiet at first, mimicking a small humming noise, only to escalate into an almost scream. But his mouth was unmoving, his lips only slightly parted, and the sight was so unsettling Nina had to look away.

Valentina put a hand on Tiana's arm, soundlessly begging for answers. For help. This didn't seem normal. And yet, what the Order had done to Jack was not normal. It couldn't be easy undoing what they did. I leaned around V and raised my eyebrows, grimacing into a plea. Tiana ignored us and spoke, despite the fact that Jack's throaty shrieking had become much louder than her voice.

"When I snap my fingers, your body will relax and your mind will be at ease, but you will retain what is currently in your mind." She snapped, and the room fell silent once more, Jack's tense extremities settling with it. His eyes closed, and there was a collective sigh of relief in the room.

Tiana fixed her gaze on Jack. "Jack, tell us about the Order of the Six. Tell us *who you are*."

A small smile slid up the side of Jack's mouth. A chill ran up my spine, because even though Jack's eyes were closed, it was clear the man sitting before me was the same guy we used to, and sometimes still did, call by his last name to show respect. It was the leader who boldly led us on a treasure hunt with all of the pompousness of a spoiled boy from a powerful family. It was the old Jack Cunningham.

"My name is Jack Cunningham," he began, his voice smooth and self-assured. "My family has been running the Order of the Six since its inception. The Order's mission is to gain total control."

"Control of what?" Nina asked, and Tiana waved a hand at her.

"Jack, what does the Order want to control?" Tiana asked, her tone just as calm as it had been before.

"Everything," he said. "And they will."

I locked eyes with Valentina, Jack's ominous words ringing in my ears.

"Jack," Tiana leaned forward. "Tell us where you've been the last three months. Before you came back to school."

Jack laughed, but there was no humor in his voice. "Receiving my punishment." His tone was cold.

"By who?"

"Who do you think? My family. The Order. Call them what you want, they're one and the same. I revealed too many family secrets, and something had to be done."

Valentina interjected. "So they messed with your memories?"

Tiana put her hand on Valentina's thigh and rephrased the question for Jack.

"Well, at least I paved the way for *something* in Order history. I was the first successful subject in their brainwashing trial. It took some time, but clearly, they were successful." His mouth was turned into a full frown now, the ice in his voice evidence he wasn't actually proud of that accomplishment.

"We should wrap this up," I whispered to Tiana, thinking that Jack had revealed enough secrets to the two strangers in the room. If he had his memories back, we could speak to him about the rest privately. But Jack spoke up, causing us all to look in his direction.

"Aren't you going to ask me what the Order wants?"

Tiana paused. "What do they want?"

Treasure, I thought. The rest of Malloy's treasure would bring them to the next level. It would be an accomplishment no others could achieve. That's what Jack had originally been looking for. It's what Allastair had punished him for leaking. But that's not what he said.

"The Order is looking for someone," he said instead, and my eyes went round. "Before I went through the brainwashing trials," Jack winced a little at the memory, and we all tensed at the sight. "Before all that," he continued, breathing through the memory, "they spent a lot of time trying to get information out of me. Information I didn't have."

"What information?" Tiana asked, anticipating our question.

"I don't know," Jack said. "But clearly, there is someone else that knows about the treasure. Someone who is a direct threat to them. Someone who could obviously take them down if the treasure was to be found and ruin everything."

"That's enough," I said in Tiana's direction, and Valentina shot me an angry look.

"Harper."

"No, she's right," Tiana pushed the metronome once more, emitting the repetitive swishing sounds. "He's been under long enough. Jack, I will count to three. When I get to three, you will wake up. *One. Two. Three.*"

At three, Jack's eyes popped open and his hands went to the armrests on the chair, clutching them for dear life. He leaned over, sucking in as much air as he could. Tiana turned off the metronome and walked over to Jack, squatting beside him and comforting him with one hand on his back. He stayed like that for a few minutes until someone spoke.

"I think we should give him some time," Sierra said, standing and ushering us to the door. Valentina was about to protest, but Jack looked up, brown hair falling into intense eyes.

"No. Stay. Now that I remember, I have some questions for the three of you." His breathing was still harsh, but it was steadier now. He squinted at Sierra and Tiana. "You can go."

I gave them an embarrassed shrug, Jack's rudeness proving once more that the real Jack was, in fact, back. But Tiana and Sierra said nothing, and simply made their way to the exit. Valentina followed them out and closed the door behind them. Their shadows filtered through the muddled window in the door as the three of them stood outside and chatted in hushed whispers.

"One of you knows something. You must," Jack said, looking between Nina and me. "For some reason, my grandfather thought *I* knew something about this missing person."

I bit my lip. "Jack, I'm really not sure what you're talking about. Everyone we know of that had anything to do with the Order is dead. Your family made sure of that," I added, clenching my jaw. "Everyone apparently, except you."

He crossed his arms. "Clearly that's not the case. *Someone* obviously eluded them, and if they think I knew, it's because of one of you three. You were in my chapter. I shared the secrets of the treasure with you, and they thought we discovered something in our search. They must think one of you told me something."

My heart rate sped up. So there was something to find after all. And the Order knew where to look. "Then why didn't Allastair kidnap us and do the same thing to us as he did to you? If he could stand to interrogate and brainwash his own family, I'm sure he'd have no qualms doing the same to us."

He smirked. "I was the prototype. You *might* be next. Who knows. But ultimately, I was chosen because I was seen as the biggest threat. For some reason, he must have thought you'd been contained to leave well enough alone. Which to be fair," he added, "is not common for my grandfather."

I thought about Rebecca's conversation with me on the beach the night Dom died. The way she'd told me she'd handled it, the implication that she'd protected me and my friends from her grandfather by dealing with things her way. Maybe she'd kept more from her grandfather than I thought.

I shook my head. "Okay, but if he thought you'd gotten information from us, that still doesn't explain why we weren't at least interrogated."

He licked his lips. "He didn't get anything out of me. I didn't know anything. He must have realized he was wrong about our chapter knowing something. But to be safe, I had to be stripped of my memories. I can't go back to being an Order leader. Not even a member," he sneered. "I guess I was too much of a risk." His eyes cut to us. "Which is exactly why you came looking for me, isn't it?"

Nina and I exchanged a glance. "Yes," I said. "And look what your family did to you. Was I wrong to think you might want to help us?"

Jack's eyebrows knit together. "I think we can help each other."

NINE

———— ❖ ❖ ❖ ————

"Let me get this straight," I said, pacing around the same empty room we'd been in for the last almost 24 hours. "You want us to help you find the person the Order is looking for. And somehow, you think that's going to give us control over the Order?"

Jack was standing in front of the window, staring out at the alleyway below us. Car horns blared up at us from the street, the ever-moving flow of traffic still ongoing into the night. "I think," he corrected, his once pressed button down now wrinkled and hanging slightly open, "the only way to truly gain control of the Order, and as a result, protect ourselves from them, is to find Malloy's hidden will."

I blinked. "How do you know there is a will?"

"Because that's what my grandfather and the others are looking for." He rolled his eyes. "Well, one of many things."

Nina nodded. "And they think that mystery person knows where it is?"

Jack's fingers tapped against his skin as he crossed his arms. "Or is hunting it down as we speak. If the Order gets to it first, they can destroy any shred of its existence. But if we get to it first, if we play it right, Harper can stake a claim on my family's money. And the rest of the Order. At least, the original amount that was taken back in the '20s."

Nina sighed. "I don't think that'll be enough."

I looked up at the ceiling, thinking. "Unless this person who knows about the will *also* has clues to find the rest of Malloy's treasure. If we work together, we can find it. That has to be enough."

Jack nodded slowly. "Right. But Harper, if we make this arrangement, there is one caveat." I waited for him to continue. "When we prove you to be the heir of the entire Malloy fortune, simultaneously stripping all money and power from my family and by default, the Order, I get half."

"What?" Nina and I balked at the same time, our voices pitching high.

"The money you recover from these endeavors, we split fifty-fifty."

Nina took a step closer to me as if her sheer presence would protect me from Jack's request. "That's ridiculous Jack and you know it. That's Fontaine money. It's Harper's. You can keep your grubby fingers off it."

Jack's face darkened. "Is it? Because I can pretend to be brainwashed for a little bit longer, play their little game, but my grandfather isn't stupid. Eventually they'll catch on and what will happen to me? If you want my help, which I suspect you do, seeing as you went through a lot of trouble to get my memories back, you'll give me my cut. How am I to protect myself when all of this goes down? By being in a better position than my family, that's how. And that means, I'm going to need the big bucks. It's the only way to ensure I get out of this alive."

Nina snorted. "Yeah, and back in power!"

He whirled on her. "Would you rather me or my family?"

Nina shrunk back and I put a hand on her shoulder. "He's right, Nina."

"What?" Nina frowned, her eyes sad. "Come on Harper, don't let him do this to you."

"We have to. And," I looked over at Jack. "Jack and I will have an alliance. We will take the Order down together. That means, both he, and I," I looked back at her, "and all of you, will be protected. That's the deal. Right Jack?" The last part was forced out between gritted teeth, but Jack nodded with a smile on his face anyway.

"That's right, Miss Fontaine."

"Great. In that case, let's start brainstorming. I'm sure your little bodyguards are going to catch on to your disappearance soon, so we'd better get together some sort of plan."

Jack waved his hand at my pocket. "Let me see that photo again. The one from Rose Island. I'm assuming you have it as well."

I pulled my cell phone from my pocket in response and dug around for the image, opening it and handing it over. Nina shuffled to Jack and looked over his shoulder.

"I don't know what good this is going to do you," Nina said. "Everyone in that photo is dead. Except for Harper, obviously." Nina winced, her insensitivity dawning on her. "Sorry."

I glanced over at Valentina's shadow. She was still chatting with the others outside the door. They must have been arranging payment details. A flicker of irritation licked up my spine. We could use Valentina for the brainstorm. Next to Jack and me, she knew the most about our family histories and the connections to the Order.

"That's you?" Jack asked, looking at me. His finger was pointed at the little girl in the photo.

"Yes. And my grandfather Nathaniel and Valentina's dad, Mr. Vasquez."

Jack *ts*ked. "I know who they are. What I don't know, however, is who is taking this picture."

I stood very still. The air felt as if it had been sucked from the room as I took in what Jack was asking.

"What, you never considered that?" Jack smiled, gleeful to be the smartest person in the room at the moment. "Look at the angle of the photo, it's clearly not on a tripod or it would be straighter. And the way you're all smiling, it looks as if someone had directed you to. Harper, you're even waving at them. You must have known them." I clenched my hands into fists to stop the shaking. I assumed I was waving at the camera, but Jack was right. Now that I really looked at it, it was clear someone else was there. Jack waved the phone at me. "*Someone* took this picture."

My voice shook. "And whoever it was knew about Rose Island. That's probably why they were all there. My grandfather and Valentina's dad had been trying to take down the Order themselves. If they brought someone with them to Rose Island, they must have been a part of it. Or they at least knew something."

"You think that's the person the Order is looking for?" Nina asked us both, but her gaze landed on me.

Jack handed me my phone, his work done. "You don't remember this day?"

My eyes were glued to the phone. "I don't remember much from that time. The only thing I do remember is—" The images of my grandfather's bloody murder splashed into my brain, temporarily mixing with images of Dom's lifeless body. I forced them to separate, focusing on the scenes from my nightmares, of Allastair confronting my grandfather Nathaniel. There was a gun. I remembered the sound of a gunshot and thought of the bullet casing I'd found in the lighthouse. Red blood oozed from Nathaniel's head.

I mentally bounced through the images until a fresh one broke through. A hand clamped over my mouth and pulled me backward. I had been there that night, watching through the crack in the door to the tunnel. And someone, Mr. Vasquez, I'd thought, had pulled me from the tunnel. Unless it hadn't been Mr. Vasquez at all. Was there a third person, someone who'd saved me that night?

I rushed over to the door Tiana was still standing behind. When I opened it, Tiana, Sierra, and Valentina all looked at me with wide eyes. I must have looked crazy or something.

"Wait, you can't leave yet. You have one more hypnotism to do."

Valentina rolled her eyes. "I don't think Jack cares if Nina does it anymore, Harper, not since he got his memories back."

I shook my head forcefully. "No, not Nina. Me." My eyes landed back on Tiana. "I want you to hypnotize me."

TEN

My sneakers slapped on cement as I walked down the street, quickening my pace. I glanced behind me to make sure no one was there. Well someone *was* there, but not Jack's bodyguards like I'd been looking for. Instead, it was Jack himself hustling to catch up to me. Valentina elbowed me hard as if to say, "do you see that?" Yes, I did see, and I also saw Nina trailing behind him, eventually slowing to a stop with her hands on her knees.

But V and I couldn't stop. We were late, apparently. A fact of which Valentina reminded me all of five minutes ago. I hadn't realized it had even gotten dark. Jack's hypnotism had taken longer than expected. My own mind-bending would have to wait.

"Hold up," Jack said, finally catching up to us. I cracked a smile. It was fun seeing all the Newport kids out of their element for once. "If you think," Jack wheezed, "I'm letting you run off before we get answers, you're out of your mind."

"Excuse me?" I quirked an eyebrow at Jack, but I didn't slow my pace. I was going to be so dead if I didn't get to the hotel on the Upper East Side in twenty minutes. Car horns beeped around us as we navigated the dark sidewalk toward the train, the bright streetlights lighting our way.

"What, so you girls get everything you want out of me, and then when we finally have a lead and you back out? Is this some ploy to use me like a dirty rag and toss me to the side?"

This time I did stop. I glanced behind Jack, but Nina was nowhere in sight. I made a mental note to send her an apology text the next chance I got.

"She's not backing out of anything, *paranoid*." Valentina crossed her arms at Jack. "Tiana has a meeting, and so do we. We will do the hypnotism. Just…not now."

I nodded and kept walking, V's explanation sufficing. "Maybe we should just take a car," I said to her, ignoring our newfound stalker.

"No way." Jack stumbled back in step with us. "I am not getting jipped out of my fifty percent."

"Fifty percent?" V asked, looking at me, but I didn't meet her eyes. Oh yeah, she'd missed that part.

I cut Jack a look. "You won't. This isn't a trick."

Jack pressed his lips together, considering this. We all slowed to a normal walking pace as I pulled out my phone and called for a car, realizing we definitely weren't going to make the train now. "Fine, then I'm going with you. You know, to be sure you make good on your promise."

I rolled my eyes. "And your little goons?" I tapped away at my phone, watching the little car icon drive down the street a block away from us.

"They'll be fine for a few more hours without me. For all they know I'm passed out in the Phi Gamma basement."

I shrugged, not sure about anything except that I had to be at a certain place at a certain time. And that time was now. A gray SUV rolled to stop in the middle of the street, turning on its hazards. I jutted my chin up at the vehicle and headed for it, indicating this was us. "I hope you're right."

When we pulled up to our destination, a doorman who had been standing in front of the building walked over to our car and opened the door for us. Valentina, Jack and I piled out, thanking the doorman with a nod.

Jack scanned the area. "Your meeting is at a hotel?"

"The Grand Ballroom to be exact," I said, giving Valentina a knowing look. "Just wait until you see what's waiting for us inside."

"Jeez, don't sound too excited," Valentina joked, looping her arm through mine and leading the way through the double glass doors. Jack trailed behind us until we reached the twelfth floor, where we stepped out of the elevator into an empty hallway. Piano music floated down the tight space and I cringed, dreading the next hour of my life.

The three of us followed the signs to the ballroom. I halted just before the doorway, peering in. Two other heads popped in beside mine, my new posse and I evaluating the shit show that was about to go down.

"Is this a...dance rehearsal?" Jack asked, incredulous. "You can dance, Harper?"

I pressed my lips into a frown. "No."

"No you can't dance, or no this isn't a dance rehearsal?"

I ignored his question, even though the answer to both was in fact, no, and redirected the conversation. "Jack Cunningham, let me introduce you to the eligible young ladies of the New York Debutante Ball." What looked like fifteen teenage girls and their male partners spun in circles as they moved across the open space, the shiny marble floor looking dangerously slippery and expensive beneath their feet.

Jack snorted. "You're kidding. This is a joke, right?" I frowned but said nothing. "Harper Fontaine? A deb?" This time, a full laugh spilled from his lips, his perfect white teeth showing.

"Shh!" I said, shoving him.

His laugh still evident in his voice, Jack added, "And you dressed like that to mingle with high society socialites?"

Valentina dug her elbow into Jack's ribs. "They're just girls."

Jack snorted again, but he was right. I looked down at my clothes and realized I was still wearing the skin-tight jeans and tank top from yesterday. When V and I crashed the Phi Gamma party, we hadn't had time to change before kidnapping Jack and dragging him to that empty office building. And we certainly hadn't had a moment to do anything else once he'd been tied to the chair. I mean, V and I were scrappy, but we weren't as strong as Jack, and we couldn't risk him waking up and overpowering one of us while the other was gone. So there we were, Valentina still in her bodycon dress and me in my clubbing outfit looking absolutely unprepared at a rehearsal for an invite-only event.

"Goddamnit." I muttered, surrendering.

Jack sighed as if the stupidity around him was too much to bear. With a roll of his eyes he started unbuttoning his white dress shirt.

"You wanna explain why you're getting naked?" V deadpanned, her eyes assessing him accusingly.

Jack sneered. "I am not *getting naked*. Here," Jack handed his shirt to me, revealing a clean white T shirt underneath. He still looked crisp as ever, his usual slacks and designer shoes enhancing the casualty of the simple top. The material waved around a bit as he shook it, forcing me to grab it from him.

"Okay, okay." I slipped the long-sleeved shirt on and started buttoning, avoiding eye contact with Jack. He was smart, I'd give him that. Now that the buttons were done up and the sleeves were rolled neatly I was starting to look like I'd worn this outfit intentionally, despite it being a tad oversized on me. I started stuffing the ends of the shirt into my jeans, but with the tight waist and extra material it was a bit of a struggle.

Jack reached out to stick his hand in the back of my pants, causing me to sway a little to dodge his touch. "Um, hello?" I whispered, my voice echoing down the quiet of the hallway, "Consent is a thing, remember?" I glanced back at the door to the ballroom and noticed the music fading as the debs finished their dance. I know boundaries had gotten a little blurred after the whole kidnapping thing, but we had to find a way to build those back up in light of our newfound friendship…or whatever this was.

"Oh please, I'm trying to *help* you."

I shot him a look. "You sound exactly like Valentina."

V protested. "Um no, I would never just touch you without asking."

My new stylist threw his hands up in mock surrender. "Okay, fine," Jack said, dripping with sarcasm. "*May I help you?*"

I hesitated. "Yes."

"Okay then." Jack shoved his hands into the lining of my pants and I looked up at V for help, but she just shrugged. My new handler pushed the white fabric down neatly and pulled the top up just slightly to create a neat, tucked look. When Jack finished, he took a step back.

"See?"

"Okay fine, so maybe you are helpful." I said, examining the smart-looking shirt.

Jack smiled and I could swear he looked...proud. Was he enjoying this?

"Harper!" An excited voice echoed into the hallway as the doorway to the ballroom opened. Shalene's wafer-like figure stepped in front of us. "There you are. *You're late,*" she chided through a smile.

"By like, five minutes," Valentina corrected.

"More like ten," Shalene narrowed her eyes, which widened the second she noticed Jack. "However, considering you brought another member from one of the Six families, I can let it slide. Jack, hello. Shalene." She introduced herself, or maybe re-introduced herself, I wasn't sure. Jack shook her hand, looking smug at her mention of him. I had to stop myself from rolling my eyes.

Shalene's grasp went to my elbow and Jacks, pulling us both into the ballroom.

"Mother, this is Harper Fontaine and Jack Cunningham." We landed in front of a short and somewhat wide woman with the same dark hair as her daughter, but hers was coiled into a neat bun. The others in the room grouped off and started chattering quietly, some of them looking in our direction as they spoke.

"Padma," Shalene's mother stuck her hand out gracefully, expecting me to shake it. I did, and with that she added, "You may call me Mrs. P."

"Nice to meet you," I said, dropping my gaze either in an attempt to show respect, or because the formalities were expressly awkward, I wasn't sure which.

"And I see you brought your date!" she cooed, and I looked behind me to see Shalene clutching Jack like he was a prize to be won. "Shalene mentioned you would, which is essential considering all the other girls met their matches at the cotillion meet-up soiree months ago."

My heart sank and I skittered up to her other side, whispering in Shalene's ear. "Valentina is my date, not Jack."

Shalene kept her focus on her mother but spoke softly in my direction so only I could hear. "Dates can only be male. You don't have to marry the guy." Panic seized at my chest, a suffocating, sinking feeling. I felt just like I had last time, trapped in a situation I wanted desperately to change. I turned around to see Valentina sitting graciously in a chair off to the side. She just shrugged, just as lost in all of this as I was.

"And that is Harper's assistant," Shalene added. I turned back to her, watching her hand wave at Valentina. As if a high schooler would have an assistant. Well, maybe in these parts they did. The pit in my stomach grew. To me she whispered, "No outside guests are allowed at these things. If you want your girlfriend here, this is how we'll have to play it off."

I took a deep breath and stared straight ahead at Mrs. P. I wasn't doing this for myself. I wasn't even doing this for my mother. I was doing this for Shalene. Which meant, I had to try and let the rest of it go.

"I think there's been some sort of mista—" Jack started, but I cut him off.

"Thank you, Shalene," I said loudly. "I'm looking forward to the ball."

Mrs. P clapped her hands. "Alright everyone! This is Harper and Jack, they will be coming out this season with the rest of you."

"Looks like someone's already done that," someone laughed under their breath, and my cheeks reddened as I spotted the brunette girl who'd said it. Mrs. P didn't seem to hear her, because she continued speaking.

"Please welcome them warmly and assist them in this process. Because they've missed the dance rehearsals, we will let them watch first, then move through the steps once more. You all could use another breakdown anyhow." The debs-to-be made a collective moaning noise and she shushed them. "Little S, come meet Harper. You'll be showing her the ropes and helping her catch up."

"Of course, mum," a girl said, slipping from the crowd to the front of the room. It was the same girl who'd made the gay joke moments ago, who I was now remembering as Little S. We'd barely crossed paths before, and she'd certainly grown up since then. Little S always looked similar to Shalene, but now she was taller and lankier. Her brown hair was chopped into a chic bob, and she wore considerably more makeup than her older sister.

"This is Little S. Her name is Shyla, but everyone calls her Little S after her big sister, Shalene," Mrs. P said, and I could tell by the way Little S's face fell that she hated that fact. That gave me a hint of pleasure after her snide comment earlier.

"Well, my work here is done," Shalene said, smiling between us. "Good job on securing a Cunningham to be your date, Harper. You've really come through for me. If you need anything else, let me know." She headed toward the exit. I waved an apprehensive hello to Little S, then caught up with Shalene before she left.

"Actually, can we use your room tonight?" I asked, and Shalene's eyebrows raised. "I mean, it doesn't have to be *your* room, but like, is there a totally private place me, Jack and V can meet up at the sorority house after this meeting? It's…kind of hard to explain." We'd shaken Jack's bodyguards for long enough. We needed a cover. It wouldn't be unreasonable for them to see Jack walking into the Delta Pi sorority house across the street. V, Tiana, and I would just need to sneak in before he gets there. That way, we could continue with my hypnotism in private, without suspicion.

Shalene tapped her fingers to her lips. "Fine. My room then. Just keep up the good work." She winked and bounced out the door, leaving me with a sick feeling in my stomach as the flowery music started up and the dancers started moving.

Jack and I took our seats next to Valentina, watching the group move silently to their respective places. I wanted to apologize to V, to tell her how much I'd wanted to do this with her, but Jack stole my attention.

"I said I wanted to come to your meeting, not join a ball. How do you suppose we keep my guard dogs from seeing us together if I have to meet you at these stupid rehearsals all the time?" he asked.

I bit my lip. "It's an upscale hotel, Jack. You're not just a frat boy, remember? Would it be that weird to be seen going into a hotel for an hour, and then leaving a couple of times a week?" To be honest, I really couldn't see Jack hooking up with some girl in the fraternity basement.

He sniffed, picking up my meaning. "I suppose not."

I waved my hand at the dancing debutantes. "And if you'd tried to leave after Shalene and Mrs. P met you, it would look a little weird. You're an adult now. You can't just creep on a dance rehearsal for a bunch of teenagers and dip. We'll have to figure out what to do once it comes time for the actual ball. Obviously the entire event is super high profile, and we might run into trouble if anyone from the Order finds out we're both in it."

A silence fell across the room, and I realized the music stopped. I sat up straighter and turned my attention to the scene in front of me.

"Harper, Jack, let's find a spot for you. Right here, in the front would be excellent," she said, dragging us in place in front of Little S and her date. In doing so she made the girl's face darken, and I suddenly realized our presence wouldn't go unnoticed without stepping on any toes. Figuratively and probably literally as well.

The dance hadn't changed much from when I'd learned it a few years ago, and Jack was working with years of waltz and ballroom training for fancy events, so we picked up the basics quickly enough to not ruffle too many feathers. We were then moved to the back temporarily, just in time to attempt our first run-through with the entire group. I was grateful Mrs. P had enough foresight to expect some mess-ups, because despite my prior knowledge of the dance, the incessant spinning and curtsying tended to get a little mixed up in my head.

The music began once more, its sound reminding me of an old movie, the kind where the young women would dance in flowing dresses and character shoes with the charming men hoping to woo them. Everyone moved all at once, two rows of couples walking in a straight line, with the women standing on the inside and the men on the outside. Each debutante held their date's hand as the male suitors rested their free hand on our waists. I held my own free hand out and mimed holding the skirts of my future dress, just as I saw the others doing. We all came to a stop, pausing for dramatic effect.

At the same time, sans Jack and I who were still one beat off, each girl took a step inward, switching hands with their male counterpart. The guys bowed as the girls dropped into a low curtsy. I stumbled a little as I fell into mine, and I was certain we all looked ridiculous doing the exact same thing to an empty room. But the debs all around me plastered on fake smiles as they allowed themselves to be spun outward toward a phantom audience, only to bow and curtsy once more. This was always my least favorite part.

The violins swirled and we all moved into a rhythm of twirling and spinning, arms crossing but never truly losing contact with our dates. I had to admit Jack's ease in guiding me across the room gave me a sliver of confidence. He dipped me when appropriate, the excited blows of drums punctuating the dramatics of each move. If I wasn't so busy attempting to keep in step with the rest of the group, I'd have feigned a gagging face to my girlfriend, who was surely getting a kick out of this whole charade.

Just when I began to get comfortable, we got to the part where we switched partners in the middle of the dance. The girl next to me spun into Jack's arms as I attempted to do the same with her date. We spun a few times in circles and then were twirled back into our original pairings. I noticed Little S staring at Jack with longing eyes across the dance floor. *Great,* I thought. Just what I need.

"Looks like someone has a little crush," I whispered, the sound inaudible to everyone but Jack under the music. Jack flicked his eyes at Little S and chuckled.

"Well, naturally." The two of us waltzed in circles across the room, and I tried not to get dizzy.

"Of course she's your type," I scoffed.

Jack made a disgusted face, his attention never breaking from me despite the prancing we were doing across this room. "What makes you think I have a type?"

My smile fell. "I don't know, she has the whole wannabe-trophy-wife thing going on. Like maybe it's her goal in life to be someone's arm candy?"

"Someone's, sure, but not mine. And aside from the fact that she's like, fifteen, Harper, I don't have a type. Attraction doesn't have a gender. At least, not to me."

I tripped a little, my ankle bending uncomfortably. Jack lifted me back up with his strong arms, helping me to avoid snapping my ankle in half. "Thanks," I muttered, but he just kept moving.

"So, what's the objective here?" he asked, and I was grateful for the subject change, feeling a little stupid about my assumptions about Jack.

"Excuse me?"

"As in, why are we doing this anyway?"

I looked down at my feet, counting my steps. "Uh, well I made a deal with Shalene. This was her condition."

"Hmm," Jack said, a surprised look on his face. "So you do come through on your agreements. Good to know."

"Of course I do."

Jack lifted my hand above my head and whirled me around, catching me with his other hand. "You know, Harper, back when we worked together on the treasure hunt I could tell you were half-assing it. Now I know it's because you were doing your own digging. The funny thing is, if we had actually worked together like I'd wanted, we might not be in this position right now."

I wanted to laugh, but I knew that would earn me a strike against Mrs. P. "What makes you say that?" I asked instead, the music coming to a crescendo in the background.

"Well my grandfather saw you as a threat, enough to keep you away from Newport to begin with. And my sister likes you, so that says a lot."

One, two, three, four. I counted my steps to the music, then glanced back up at Jack. "Again, I know you missed it, but your sister killed my best friend and got my other friend almost arrested for murder. Hardly seems like that qualifies as her being affectionate."

Jack hummed. "Ah, so she really does like you then. Interesting…" I looked at him, aghast. He chuckled. "She didn't have you killed, did she?"

I wanted to dissect this further, but the music mercifully came to a stop. The room's spinning didn't end, however, and apparently Jack noticed, because he kept his arm looped through mine as we waited for feedback from Mrs. P.

She clapped politely and the rest of the room followed suit, a quiet sound that ended as quickly as it started.

"This is cotillion, people! You are all making your debut, act like it! Harper and Jack, excellent job for your first rehearsal. We will pick this up again next time. Little S," she said, redirecting her attention to her daughter. "Don't forget to assist Harper with the small details. Glove measurements, dresses, tiaras, you know the drill." I winced at the word "tiaras". She nodded and the room disbursed.

When I felt confident enough to walk by myself again, I left Jack behind to greet Little S properly. Her back was turned to me, so I tapped her on the shoulder. "Hi, I'm Harper." I walked up to her, my friendliest grin on my face despite my exhaustion from the past couple of days. "I really appreciate you taking the time to—"

"Harper, is it?" Little S whirled around, crossing her arms. "I would welcome you, but I don't find it appropriate that my mother and the board decided to bring two new people into the season when we're mere weeks away from cotillion. A debutante ball takes *months* of preparation. The invites were already sent out, and they certainly didn't include you. I'm not sure why my sister would advocate for you, but that doesn't exactly give you points in my book either." Little S tucked her hair behind her ear. "Stay out of my way and you might get through this."

My lips parted. I was not about to go head-to-head with a girl almost three years younger than me. This whole thing was insane. I was only here because her sister thought it would help her, but apparently Shyla didn't share the sentiment. I was about to say as much when Little S's entire expression morphed into a grin as sweet as molasses.

"Jack Cunningham, hello," she said, offering a hand like she wanted him to kiss it. I rolled my eyes. "Lovely to have you with us."

"Thank you, you as well." Jack responded, and I held back a gag. He loved every second of this. I caught Valentina's eyes across the room and waved her over.

"Can we go?" Jack asked, holding up a bare arm, goosebumps noticeable on his flesh. "It's getting a little nippy in here, and I want my shirt back."

I ignored him and slipped my hand in Valentina's as she approached us. "Let's go," I said. "I think I'd rather have a psychologist poke around inside my brain than be mindfucked by Shalene's little sister." Valentina raised her eyebrows at that, and I waved her off. "Don't worry about it. We have bigger fish to fry."

ELEVEN

"We are going to approach this hypnotism a little bit differently," Tiana said, sitting in Shalene's makeup chair. I was resting on the queen-sized bed across from her. My back was pressed against the plush headboard, my legs sticking straight out as I hugged one of the sorority girl's throw pillows. Nina and Valentina sat on the edge of the mattress, both anxiously hunched in my direction. Jack was the only other person in the room, his arms and legs crossed in his usual casual posture. Shalene had given us our privacy in her space, which was good, considering I was certain I wouldn't have been able to explain this to her.

"Well this is rich," Jack uncrossed his feet at the ankles, then crossed them again. "I was tied to a chair but Harper Fontaine gets the royal treatment for *her* hypnotism."

I rolled my eyes. Tiana interjected. "I didn't mean the setup would be different, I meant the technique. Though, I won't be using a metronome, like I did for you, Jack. Harper, you said you're a visual learner? We'll be using this to hypnotize you instead." A long silver necklace jingled as it fell from her hand, dangling in front of her, a silver pendulum attached to the bottom.

I nodded, and she continued. "For Jack, we were bringing his subconscious to the front of his mind, opening it, and releasing his memories more generally, so to speak." Tiana waved her left hand about slowly as she explained, allowing the information to penetrate our understanding. "But for you, we are attaching ourselves to a specific memory. In some ways, that's much easier, especially since you already have had some recollection of this event in your dreams."

The weight of what I was about to do leached into the corners of my brain. I needed to remember the night of my grandfather's death, to *really* remember it. If there had been a third person on the island that night, I could identify them, and our search could truly begin. Right now, that idea was all we had. I nodded again, swallowing the lump in my throat.

Tiana stared at me another moment. "Are you sure you want to do this?" Valentina's hand stuck out and landed on my shin. She gave me a squeeze. I didn't look at her.

"Yes."

Tiana nodded this time, raising the pendulum once more and giving it a little shake. The heavy metal swung side to side, slowly at first, then settled into a consistent rhythm. A subtle *whoosh*ing sound pinged back and forth. "Now Harper, keep your eyes on the moving object. Focus only on this. Allow the rest of the world to melt away. Breathe in, and out."

I did as she said, letting the air move into every inch of my body. In a great release I let it all go slowly, air blowing out of my pursed lips like a pierced balloon. Eventually, my awareness began slipping away, and somewhere in my consciousness I knew it was happening. I let it.

A voice called to me - it was Tiana, I reminded myself as my eyes closed, settling deeper into relaxation. "I am going to count down from three.

With each number, your present self slips away, and you will find yourself at the Rose Island Lighthouse, just as you were when you were six. When I hit one, you will be in a trance, but you may still communicate with me."

A heaviness washed over me, the feeling of sleep so imminent and yet so far away.

"Three." My eyes danced under my closed lids, darkness the only thing I took in before me.

"Two." Her words beckoned me deeper, and I followed.

"*One.*"

My heart suddenly crashed against my ribs. I could see my hands reaching for a door. They were impossibly small. Someone pulled my hand away from the brass knob, pinning it to my side and pressing their finger to my lips with their other hand, shushing me. I gave in and stayed silent. And then the voices began. I moved to the door, pushing my ear against it, and the presence behind me followed.

"You thought I wouldn't find out?" It was an angry voice. A man. Another person spoke, and the sound was so familiar I wanted to cry out to them. But the same hand that shushed me once shushed me again, and instead, I broke away from their grip just enough to shuffle to the tiniest crack between the door and the wall. It was barely there, a sliver really, but big enough that my tiny eye could see the man that had practically raised me. My grandfather.

"Of course not. I'm not the fool you believe me to be." White hair paired with a matching mustache peered back at me. My grandfather was tall, and strong for his age. But just then, he looked so much smaller. A moment later, I realized why. I'd never seen one in real life. It was the stuff of movies, or video games. But this was real. A shiny metal gun came into view, followed by the gray hair of a man I'd crossed paths with many times. Allastair Cunningham.

"I don't believe you to be a fool, Nathaniel. Quite the opposite, in fact." As I heard Allastair's words echo in my head, something prompted me from somewhere out of reach. I replied, repeating my grandfather's name just as Allastair had. *Nathaniel.* For a moment, I was unclear whether it was my own voice—my real adult voice—or the memory of Allastair that was speaking. For a brief moment, it had been both.

"Which is exactly the problem," he continued, taking a step forward, his gun pointed directly at my grandfather. "I warned you. I tried to keep you out of this."

"You tried to keep me submissive," Nathaniel corrected, taking a step toward the weapon. His boldness made him appear braver than the fear that showed clearly in his eyes, even from where I was standing.

Allastair leaned off to the side and picked something up, then brought it into view in my tiny field of vision. A large leather-bound book, the color as black as the night sky. He waved it with his free hand.

"You failed, Nathaniel. You wanted my ledger, what, so you could expose me? Expose the Order? If you wanted to stop us, it was going to take a lot more than a list of people we've killed. If you thought that would be enough proof, you were wrong. I'm sorry to say, old friend, but it's too late for you. If you tell me who else was involved, your family will live."

My grandfather didn't move, his face as hard as stone. "Keep my family out of this. They don't know anything."

"I know you've been to Rose Island. With the girl. Who else knows about the treasure?" Allastair took another step toward Nathaniel, who stepped back instinctively, the fireplace blocking him from moving away any further. He was cornered.

Nathaniel shook his head, the mention of me breaking his facade just a little. His voice shook the tiniest bit when he spoke. "Harper is too young. She doesn't understand. Please, Allastair. We were friends once."

The gray-haired man shook his head solemnly. "We were. And that's why I'll leave her be. For now." Allastair leaned slightly out of my window of vision. "Here," he said to someone else, the gun passing from his hand to somewhere I couldn't see. "Do it."

"Allastair, please," my grandfather pleaded.

Allastair shook his head again, as if he'd caught a child stealing candy, rather than his friend double-crossing him. "Harper is young, like you said. She'll bounce back."

"No, please—"

"We're adding another name to the list tonight," The old Cunningham said, waving the black book in his left hand. My grandfather's hands went up, one hand blocking his chin, the other hovering straight out in front of his chest. A crackling blast went off as a bullet shot into view, and within the span of less than a second spiraled directly toward my grandfather, the force throwing him backward. The next part happened slowly, so slowly in fact that I no longer felt like I was living inside the memory. Instead, I stood over the scene watching, like a puppeteer in a nightmare. But I was not in control.

A hard crack split my ears as Nathaniel's body hit the floor, crimson blood pooling quickly around his head, his white hair stained by his death forevermore. The man with the gun took a step forward, blocking the body from view. I clocked the tan skin and blonde hair I'd more recently been getting to know. A sound escaped from my lips, but not here, not in this world. In my real world. But it didn't matter, I didn't hear it. Because in the same moment a hand clamped over my mouth, and I jumped back into my six-year-old body, somehow now both watching and living the moment at the very same time.

Gold rings were stacked on the aging hand, and it occurred to me finally that it had been a woman's hand the entire time. I felt myself being pulled backward down the tunnel. My teeth bit my lip at the force of the woman's hand on my mouth, urging me to stay quiet. I swallowed the taste of blood, a scream desperate to burst from my lips. But I already felt like I was screaming. And somewhere else, I had been.

After a few moments of struggle the woman picked me up and pressed my head to her chest, muffling the sounds I attempted to make. I felt my body jostle as she moved quickly through the tunnel back toward Castle Hill. When we reached the split between Malloy's handmade tunnel and the rocks that formed the sea cave running another half-mile to the Castle Hill Lighthouse, the woman released my head, still carrying me in her arms, allowing me a moment of relief. But I didn't scream. I didn't cry either. The young version of me simply stared straight ahead, something in the back of my mind already beginning to repress the terrible scene I'd just encountered.

And that's when I saw it. Attached to the right shoulder of the woman who'd protected me was a large ruby pin inches from my face, a cluster of shiny red stones and diamonds forming what looked almost like a rose. I reached out and touched it, my fingers grazing over the sharp gems that were illuminated by the moonlight shining through the cracks in the cave.

Someone began counting far off in the distance, and I started to see the pin with my own eyes more clearly, leaving the six-year-old girl in the arms of the woman.

I tried to narrow back in on the item, eager to keep focus on it. Something about it was special, that I knew for certain. I'd never seen anything like it. It was so impressive, so unique to me that I wondered how I'd ever forgotten it in the first place. But I would not forget again. Because although I still could not see the woman's face, I now knew that the third person we were looking for was, in fact, a woman. And if we could find the owner of this pin, we might be able to get some answers.

"*One.*" Tiana's voice registered as my eyes popped open. I blinked a few times, taking in my surroundings. I was not on Rose Island or running back to Castle Hill in someone's arms. I was in Shalene's bedroom in a sorority house. And Valentina was crying.

Nina's hand rubbed her back absently as her eyes darted from her friend to me with desperation, or maybe worry, filling her eyes.

"V?" I asked, shooting up in the bed. My voice came out as almost a croak, and I realized I must have actually screamed earlier, when I'd imagined it. It sure felt like it. But that wasn't my problem right now. My girlfriend was on her knees on the floor, her hands covering her face as she took hard breaths. Panic seized my stomach, and I considered that there must have been something else, something I must have shared with the group that I'd missed. But whatever it was, it was killing Valentina.

"Does...does she know the woman?" I asked Nina, wondering how much I'd shared with everyone during my memory replay.

Nina shook her head. "No, Harper. Not a woman. You..." she glanced down at Valentina, hesitating.

"What?"

"It was Valentina's dad." She whispered that last part. "You said, 'Mr. Vasquez' when we asked who was holding the gun. When we asked who…"

"I'm so sorry Harper, I'm sorry." The sound of feet pounding followed Valentina as she stood up abruptly and bounded out of the room. I scrambled to my feet and ran toward the door, but it was Jack that stepped in front of me.

"I would give her a minute," he said, not necessarily sympathetically but not coldly either.

I waved my hand toward the door. "She's distraught, Jack, I have to make sure she's okay."

"She isn't, Harper." Nina stood up off the edge of the bed and put one hand on my arm. "She just found out her dad *didn't* save you from the tunnel, like you guys thought. He was the one that killed your grandfather."

Jack smirked. "Turns out it wasn't my good old granddaddy after all. What a twist." My hand shot out and slapped Jack across the face, a loud cracking sound echoing cleanly throughout the room. He stumbled back, rosy heat already spreading across his soft skin.

"Not that I don't love being slapped for the *second time today*," Jack growled, the humor from his previous statement gone, "but need I remind you all that I'm *on your side?*" He pressed a hand hard against his angular jaw, babying his cheek.

"Mr. Vasquez must have been a double agent for Allastair or something," Nina continued, ignoring the face-off between me and Jack. "And then, I don't know, based on what you guys told me about all this, it kind of sounds like maybe he was found out all those years later, when Valentina was fourteen, and was also murdered by the Order. I mean, I'm guessing, at least. Why else would they kill him?"

I shook my head, the seriousness of what I'd just revealed slapping me harder than I'd hit Jack. "No, no, no…" I muttered, pushing my fingers into my hair. "No! I wouldn't have done this if I'd known!"

Tiana stood up and put her hand on my shoulder. Her kind face was turned down into a sad smile. "This is why we are careful about doing things like this. Sometimes getting the truth is too much."

"Oh hogwash," Jack countered, dropping his hand from his face as if forgetting about it, the bed bouncing as he sat on it casually. "We have a lead. Who is the woman, Harper? You didn't give us a name."

"Are you British now?" Nina crossed her arms at Jack. He waved away her criticism.

"I don't know her name. I didn't see her face either."

"Goddamnit," Jack cursed.

I turned to him. "But I did see a unique-looking pin. It was covered in rubies and diamonds, and looked kind of like a rose." My hand went up to the invisible image of the pin I was attempting to conjure in front of me, pointing to the details as I pulled them from my brain. "It was extravagant, the kind of thing you'd only wear if it was important or special to you in some way, or maybe to a fancy event. It's not the kind of thing most people keep in their jewelry boxes. Does that ring a bell to anyone?" My hand dropped. I looked between Nina and Jack, hoping someone who'd lived in Newport their whole life may have caught a glimpse of it once.

Nina shook her head, but Jack looked thoughtful. "Jack?"

"If it's precious jewelry we need to find, I think I know where we need to go."

I glanced at Nina, who shrugged.

He waved a finger between Nina and me. "But obviously I can't go, and Thing 3 is M.I.A., so I suppose it'll just be the two musketeers on this one."

I sighed. He was right. "Fine. Tell us where we need to go."

TWELVE

"I wish Valentina was here," Nina said, saying exactly what I was thinking. I met her eyes as we stood across the street from the nameless hole-in-the-wall jewelry shop in Queens the next morning, hands in our pockets and confidence left back in Manhattan. I frowned, and Nina added sheepishly, "Sorry. It's true though. We need her shameless bravery. Jack said to be careful with this guy. Whatever that means."

I sighed. "No, you're right. I wish she was here too. She's been avoiding me since the hypnotism yesterday." My mind almost drifted off to a dark place, but I shook it off. "Are we even sure this is where Jack meant?"

Nina flashed the GPS app on her phone at me. "You tell me. This is the address Jack gave us." She hiked her purse strap higher on her shoulder. "You don't think this could be a setup, do you? Like maybe he knew who the woman with the pin was already and he's just trying to get rid of us somehow, now that he doesn't need us?"

I scanned the street in front of me as I thought. A hot dog truck and an ice cream truck were situated inconspicuously down the street, gathering a small cluster of customers. The road was lined with parked cars, a few hovering with their hazards on in front of storefronts on this busy street. But this corner of the street was significantly less active, with a couple shops locked up, their graffitied roll down gates either pulled down for the day, or possibly forever, collecting dust nearby. No one went in or out of the storefront we were supposed to be walking into any second.

"What's he going to do, have us murdered? In broad daylight?" I asked, playing it off like a joke. But somewhere deep down, I wondered if that was possible. Instead I said, "Besides, if Jack was planning to get rid of us, he wouldn't have tried so hard to earn his place with us. I mean, you should have seen him waltzing at the deb rehearsal." Nina's lips pursed. "Sorry about ditching you, by the way. We were super late. Otherwise, we would've waited," I offered, not wanting to take our friendship rekindling for granted. She shrugged.

"Well, if we're going to do this. Let's just do it. Yeah?" Nina bit her lip, her question sitting in her eyes.

I waved her on. "Let's go."

A chime went off as I pushed open the heavy solid door, signaling to the store's owner that we'd just entered. I didn't want to be first walking into the lion's den, but I could tell Nina was scared. Someone had to take charge, and in this case, I guessed it was me. I fought the urge to yell hello, hoping to glimpse the man we were looking for first. My shoulders grazed the shelves on either side of me, careful not to bump the glass cases too hard. The space was tinier on the inside than it had looked, and despite the gleaming jewelry littered intentionally throughout the display cases, there was barely enough space to get a really good look at anything.

"Who is it?" a strong Russian accent echoed from somewhere out of sight. Nina and I both yelped in surprise, jumping a little bit and bumping into one another. I put my hand over my heart to steady it, looking back at Nina and then around the room in the search of the sound of the voice.

When we didn't answer quickly enough, the man spoke again. "I said, who is it?"

"Uh," I began, craning my neck around the shelf blocking the hallway that seemed to lead deeper into the store.

"Back here," he said, "If you are in the right place, that is."

Hesitantly, Nina and I slipped around the shelf and found ourselves looking at an open doorway, an even tinier office nestled inside. A burly man with a balding head sat at his desk, and though I'd never seen "The Godfather", the way he poised behind his workstation like a man in charge made me feel like I could be watching that movie. In one hand was what looked like a specialized magnifying glass, and in the other was a small diamond.

"We're looking for a jeweler." I said, my voice steady despite my fast-beating heart.

The man lowered the tools in his hand and kept his gaze between us. "You've found one."

When he said nothing else I continued, this entire encounter painfully awkward. "We need help finding a pin. Or more specifically, a woman that might have owned, or still does own, this particular pin."

The jeweler paused, then held up the diamond again, squinting one eye as he examined it through his tiny magnifying glass. "Who sent you?" he asked, his "o"-sounds clipped and short, his attention still on the task at hand.

I paused, wondering how much to give. If we didn't tell this guy who sent us, he probably wasn't going to help us.

"Jack Cunningham."

The man froze, arms still holding up his tools, and glanced up at us. His eyes flicked between us. "A Cunningham, huh?"

"Mhm," Nina said, nodding eagerly.

The diamond was placed back in its box and the magnifying glass set down on the table as we earned the jeweler's full attention. "Tell me about this pin," he said, intertwining his fingers in front of him on the desk.

"Um...so it's a large pin, definitely expensive."

"Sit," the man said, his accent heavy, waving to the empty chairs on the other side of the desk. I cleared my throat at the interruption, but did as I was told. Nina and I wiggled past each other to squeeze into the antique-looking chairs. Even with the large desk between us and the man, he still felt a little too close.

"Right, so it looks like a rose, kind of, and it's made from rubies and diamonds."

I watched as the jeweler pulled a clean sheet of paper from a stack of files and began sketching. Nina and I watched in awe as he quickly formed something similar to what I'd described. He pushed it toward me and asked, "Something like this?"

I shuffled in my seat. "Yeah, almost." I pointed to a few small details that weren't exactly right, and when he'd finished fixing them, he held up the drawing.

"Okay, I see. This is a unique piece. I will make some calls. Give me two days and come back. I will have an answer for you and you will have a big check for me. Cunningham knows the rate."

Before I could ask the man if he needed my phone number, or exactly what the rate was that Jack usually paid him, he glanced back up at us. "Goodbye."

Nina and I shot up from our seats, eager to get the hell out of there. We mumbled our thank-you's and were back on the hot sidewalk before we even registered what had happened. Cars whirred by, drowning out Nina's words beside me. "Did Jack's lead actually come through for us?"

"It sounds like he just might. Two days. That's all we need. In two days, we should have the name of the woman who could change everything."

THIRTEEN

---◆◆◆---

"Excuse me?" Mrs. P's voice boomed through the open doorway to the ballroom and reached Nina and I down the hall of the hotel. I smoothed down my hair and tried to collect myself before facing the woman's wrath, knowing I'd probably look better if I'd gotten more than a few hours of sleep.

Last night was unbearably lonely without Valentina, whose simple "I'm sorry" texts did little to make me feel better, knowing she was probably suffering with the news of her father, and that there was very little I could do about it. When the texts became shorter and less frequent I decided to give her some space, knowing V probably had to work through this alone. I was way too wrapped up in the whole thing and my guess was, she needed her family.

I was grateful to have Nina, at least. She was kind enough to sleep over at my place instead of at her hotel last night. Maybe the jeweler thing freaked her out, or maybe she knew she only had a few more days here before her parents returned from their trip, but either way, I was glad she decided to come with me to rehearsal today.

I snorted and whispered to Nina, who was walking next to me. "Boy am I glad that's not me. When you meet Mrs. P, you'll understand why it's better to just drift into the background. Years of directing events has somehow made her vocal cords even louder. I feel bad for the fool who—" And then I stepped inside and saw who Mrs. P was directing her outrage at. "Shit," I added, noticing Jack standing confidently in front of her.

"Uh, you mean that fool?" Nina joked, pointing at Jack, and I ignored her, hustling over to Jack's side.

Mrs. P barely acknowledged my presence, keeping her focus on Cunningham. "You expect me to replace you a week before the ball, after I graciously accepted you as such a late entry? You *must* be joking." Her eyes were narrowed into slits.

I panicked, grabbing Jack's elbow and pulling him out of earshot. "I'm sorry Mrs. P, give us a minute, okay?"

"Harper Fontaine, you've certainly gotten comfortable getting handsy with me these days, haven't you," Jack said, not bothering to explain what Mrs. P was talking about.

"Jack, do you wanna tell me what happened back there?" I asked quietly through gritted teeth. "What the hell is she talking about, *replacement?*"

Jack pointed to a tall, sophisticated young man around our age, maybe a little older, standing a few feet from Mrs. P with his hands in his pockets. In all the chaos I hadn't noticed him. "Edward Belkin. He's one of my fraternity brothers. He's from a good family in Connecticut. Of course, not as notable as mine or yours, but he'll do."

I shook my head as Nina shuffled up to us. "No, Jack, I mean, you can't just *quit*. I thought we were in this together?"

Jack crossed his arms. "No, we're in the treasure hunt together," he whispered, leaning in. "We're doing the whole, Order takedown together. Nowhere in that agreement did I sign up for cotillion."

"I thought we said we'd figure it out!"

"Figure out what?" Nina asked, sticking her head into our newly formed triangle.

Jack lifted his fingers, examining his perfectly manicured nails. "My grandfather, or someone else in the Order finding out I'm doing this. We agreed we'd deal with it later, but Harper, it's *later*. I heard Mrs. P talking about sending our families invitations to the debutante ball. Family, meaning mine. Even without invites, the Order knows everything. There's no way around it. I can't do the ball without them finding out."

Nina bit her lip., "And if they find out, they'll realize you're involved too, Harper, and our cover is blown. They'll know something is up. Maybe not that we undid all the brainwashing, but *something*. Jack's right."

I cut Nina a look. She shrugged as if to apologize for taking Jack's side. I pressed my fingers to my hairline. "Okay but, this ball can't just blow up. My participation is supposed to, I don't know, elevate the whole thing, not make it a huge mess." The thought that I could make any event any cooler seemed insane to me, especially considering the complications I continued to make for it. Still, it's what Shalene wanted, so I added, "I owe Shalene."

A sigh escaped from my tense lips. "I thought they already sent invitations months ago. As long as no one gossiped about it, your family shouldn't find out until *after* the ball. And by then, hopefully, we'd already have found our mystery woman."

"That's a lot of *if's* Harper," Nina said. I cut her another glare. "I'm sorry! You're not thinking clearly because you're in a tight situation. Who cares if that Edmund guy takes Jack's place? Just let him do it, go to the ball and get it over with."

"Edward," Jack corrected her.

"Whatever," Nina responded.

I turned to stare at Edward, who looked far too put together to be spending his days at a frat house.

"Wait," Jack rubbed his chin, assessing me. "You *want* me to be your date. This is about me, isn't it?"

I shoved him a little, just enough to make him sway on his feet but not enough to get Mrs. P's attention. We'd had enough of that. I noticed Little S eyeing us across the expansive ballroom, however, and averted my own eyes the second ours met.

I grimaced. "Absolutely not. It's just easier with you. Now he has to learn the whole dance in a matter of days and he could easily screw anything up."

"Harper, *we* learned the dance in a matter of days."

I put my hands on my hips. "Everyone is already waiting for me to make another mistake again. At least with you I knew things would go smoothly."

Cunningham's cocky grin softened. "I'll teach him the dance."

"Fine. But then you're responsible for making sure he's prepared with everything. His tux, knowing where to be and when. I don't care if you have to pay him or babysit him, you're responsible."

Jack gave me a condescending pat on the shoulder that did little to curb my worry. "Fine." With that, he turned and headed back to Mrs. P, Nina and I following closely behind.

"As I said Padma," Jack said, using Mrs. P's full first name for dramatic effect, "I'm eternally sorry I must miss the ball. But as it happens, I couldn't say no to the Queen."

Mrs. P's head snapped back up in surprise a little, her eyes wide and intrigued. I bit back a scowl at the lie. "The…Queen?"

"Oh yes. She's having another garden party, and I must go represent my family. You understand. Edward here is fully up to the job. You must be aware of the Connecticut Belkins, I'm sure. Their family has a wonderful reputation." Mrs. P nodded thoughtfully, her mind probably still on the Queen's fictitious garden party.

"Certainly," Mrs. P managed to say and then, realizing her frazzled state, shook it off and straightened. "I will get Edward registered." Then, to the rest of the room: "Alright everyone, rehearsal is starting. We are down to the wire now, everyone!" Once she noticed Nina, however, her tone changed. "Who are you?"

I considered what Shalene said about no outside visitors being allowed. Before I could make up an excuse, Jack, of all people, came to the rescue. "She's my assistant, Maeve." Nina made a pained expression but nodded anyway.

"Finc," was all Mrs. P said.

"*Maeve?*" I heard Nina whisper to Jack as he met up with her, leaving Edward and me standing awkwardly in place.

"Of course," he explained. "I always imagined my assistant to have an awful name. It's kind of a rite of passage."

Before I could take a breath, I was back in my usual dance position, but instead of Jack holding my waist, a different snobby college boy took his place. I gave Edward an awkward smile and I watched Jack and Nina take some empty seats off to the side of the room in observance.

When the music began, I realized Edward didn't know one single step of the dance, because we immediately crashed into each other. Mrs. P waved at the pianist to stop playing and shuffled over to us. "Okay, this isn't working. You two, step off to the side and work on the dance as the rest rehearse. It seems Edward has some catching up to do." Her mouth was pressed into a tight scowl, so I didn't protest.

The two of us moved out of the way of the other dancers, and I attempted to show Edward some of the moves as the rest of the group started up again with the music. It seemed like he was finally catching on when someone rammed into my back hard, knocking me onto the floor.

A little *oof* sound dropped from my lips and I hit the ground, palms and knees first, the air evacuating my lungs.

"Oops," a snotty voice said sarcastically. "My bad." I looked up to see Little S glaring at me. I set my jaw. That bitch really had it out for me. I wasn't even dancing with Jack anymore and she still had a problem with me.

"No, no, no!" Mrs. P yelled, scrambling over to me. "Harper, why don't you, Edward, and Jack go home and teach Edward the dance before our next rehearsal. You're getting in the way of the others." My face flushed and I nodded, the three of us and Nina heading silently to the exit.

I didn't find a quiet place to rehearse with them. My nerves were shot for the day and I didn't feel like jumping through hoops to avoid Jack's bodyguards, so

I left the boys to rehearse themselves with Nina's oversight, much to her pleasure, and went home.

What I saw when I arrived, however, was not what I'd expected. Puffy white gowns were strewn about the medium-sized apartment, our fancy sofas and shiny tables covered in fabric. My mom excelled at the "less is more" approach to decorating, choosing minimalist centerpieces for the tables or carefully selected art for the walls. But now, with the chaos of the dress piles, our sleek home looked more like a dress shop on Madison Avenue.

My eyebrows knit together. "Um, mom?" I shouted. Her head popped out from a nearby doorway.

"Harper!" My mother stepped out and approached me, her blue slacks and neatly tucked blouse making me wonder how comfortable she could possibly be hanging around the house in her usual business casual. Sure, she had excellent taste, but we never exactly saw eye to eye on what constituted as appropriate, or at the very least, comfortable. I certainly didn't expect our taste in dresses to match up either.

"Is someone getting married?" I asked, my attempt at a joke as I waved at the gowns, but the flashbacks of the most recent wedding I'd attended started slipping into my consciousness—Valentina's mom screaming, her hands to her cheeks in her own white dress. The images pressed behind my eyes, which watered at the thought. I blinked a few times and narrowed in on the present, staring intently at the lacy creams and whites sitting before me.

My mom picked up a nearby dress off the side of the couch and held it up, as if to display its beauty. "No silly, they're for you." She smiled a bright smile, a perfect set of even teeth gleaming. "I heard about the debutante ball!" she squealed, and my stomach dropped. I completely forgot I'd have to explain this to my mom. But then again, seeing how pleased she was at this unfolding, maybe this could work in my favor. "I'm so glad you decided to get involved in something, honey. This will be so good for you. It will keep you busy."

I nodded my head, pretending to agree with her, my eyes scanning the tulle.

"Just, be sure not to let it get in the way of your schoolwork," she added, leaning up against the couch and lowering the gauzy fabric. I rolled my eyes.

"Mom."

"Well, I know you haven't even started. It doesn't even look like you've touched it since we last talked. Honestly Harper, Valentina finished her work for the week before she left."

My throat tightened. "She...she left?"

My mom frowned, a brown strand of hair slipping from her neat bun and falling around her eyes. "Oh, I'm sorry my love, she didn't tell you? I just assumed she was visiting her brother for a few more days."

I gnawed at the inside of my cheek. "Did...did she say that? That she's going to be back in a few days?" My mother stood up and placed the heavy dress back on the couch, the fabric making a rustling sound. Her hand went to the side of my face and brushed a few strands of hairs away.

"Did you have a fight? I didn't realize."

"No," I took a quick step back, protesting the idea. "We're fine. She must have just forgotten to mention it. That's all. I know she misses Adan." I forced a smile and headed to my room as quickly as I could manage without concerning my mother. My life was very quickly falling to pieces all over again, and the one person who always helped me put it together, was gone.

FOURTEEN

———— ◆◆◆ ————

My stomach clenched, the sweet and spicy smells of mustard and ketchup sitting on the untouched hot dog in my hand now making me feel a little sick. My phone rang endlessly against my ear with no one picking up on the other end. I'd been craving a hot dog all morning, but now that I was back here on that same street in Queens where our only lead was stationed at with only Nina by my side and my girlfriend not answering her phone, I lost my appetite. Nina, on the other hand, had scarfed down her own hot dog and ordered another without a second thought.

I ended the call and dialed Valentina once more. The empty ringing blasted through my ears as Nina said, "I'll give you a minute," taking a bite from the food poised in her hand and pacing slowly in the direction of the jeweler mere feet away.

"Come on, V, talk to me," I muttered, turning my back to Nina and staring blankly at the street. The phone went to voicemail and I hung up, shoving my phone in my pocket and scanning the corner for a trash can to swallow my wasted lunch. Before I could find one, Nina's voice called my name, the urgency behind it so unsettling that goosebumps raised on my arms.

"Nina?" I asked, jogging up to her and looking her over, flashes of blood appearing and disappearing on her dress, the same way I'd seen them splattered on her the day Dom had died. But she wasn't holding Adan in her arms like she had then, Dom's blood transferred from Adan's own clothes to hers. She wasn't even wearing a dress. And she wasn't looking at me either. I followed her gaze to the jeweler's storefront inches from us, the glass door revealing what was inside. The sight was enough to cause the hot dog to slip right from my hand and onto the hot concrete.

"No...no...no...no!" I yelled, my hands going to the handle and shaking it open, the heavy door not budging.

"Harper?" Nina asked meekly, as if I somehow held the answers.

"Oh god, please no!" I shouted under my breath, looking around for something, anything around us. A loose brick beckoned to me from the side of the building and I pressed my fingers around it, pulling hard. It didn't budge, so I stood and kicked it with my boots a few times, hearing a grinding noise as the slab loosened just enough. I stuck my fingers around its edges once more and yanked hard, almost falling back onto my butt but catching myself as the brick released from captivity.

"Harper!" Nina shouted, this time her words bearing meaning. I knew there was a chance someone might hear the commotion and catch me. But I didn't care. This was a small concern compared to the massive, life-changing events that were happening around me. People were dying, and we had one lead. So I ignored Nina and the warning bells going off in my head.

I heaved the heavy brick into the air and threw it as hard as I could at the glass door, the brick quickly bouncing off the hard surface and crumbling to the ground, mostly intact. Nina managed to jump out of harm's way. The glass had made a small cracking sound on impact, but the door did not shatter. I picked up the brick and thwacked the edge again and again on the same splintering spot. Before the crack could widen, Nina's hands circled my wrist, holding the arm that was yielding the heavy object. I froze, looking back at her, eyes wide in a kind of trance.

"Harper," Nina said quietly this time, finally holding my attention. "We don't need to get inside. We can see from here. Look."

She released me and I lowered my hand, taking a step closer to the shiny glass. I pressed my forehead to it, offering a bit of shade to dampen my own reflection looking back at me. The dark space came into view, illuminated by the sun bouncing off empty glass shelves—a very different transparent material than the hundreds of diamonds that used to litter their surfaces. It was clear from here. The entire place had been cleaned out.

A loud alarm blared above us, the quick beats of sound matching the rhythm of my heart. We jumped.

Nina grabbed my elbow, pulling me away, but I hesitated a second longer.

I squinted my eyes to try and catch sight of the office, just to make sure. I couldn't see much from the angle we were standing at, but I didn't need to to know that it was also empty. The corner of the large wooden desk in my view lay bare, every file and object obviously packed and long gone. The jeweler had left. And he'd taken our only lead with him.

FIFTEEN

---◆◆◆---

"He's gone, Jack. The jeweler is gone! The entire place is empty," I yelled into my phone, Nina and I a safe distance from the shop now, sitting inconspicuously on a park bench a few blocks away as the alarm continued to blare faintly from somewhere down the street.

"No," he said, the shock in his voice proving to me for the first time that he hadn't known about this.

"Yes, Jack. And he knows who we're looking for. Who is this guy anyway? What would he want with that information? And why wouldn't he just pass it along to us for the paycheck, isn't that what he does?"

A loud sigh cut through the speaker. "Oh god. I'm so stupid. Of *course*."

"Jack!" I yelled, drawing the attention of a handful of passersby—a cyclist, a girl walking her dog and a couple included.

"I'm sorry," he moaned. "But I get it now. My guy doesn't want the information. He won't do anything with it." I shook my head, even though he couldn't see me. "I don't know if he found who we were looking for. He certainly passed the information along. But not to us. To someone else for a much larger paycheck. To my grandfather."

"What?" Nina yelled this time, her face drawing close to my phone receiver. "This dude was an Order connection?!"

Loud breathing came from Jack's end. "I know, I'm sorry. I just...*all* of my connections are Order connections. I didn't think about it."

I wanted to scream. We'd just dropped the most important information we have in the Order's lap. Even if the jeweler didn't figure out who the woman with the pin was, we'd still made her a target. Very possibly, the only person who knows about the Order that isn't sucked into its circle is out there with a bullseye on her back now. And it was because of us.

"What does this mean?" Nina asked, her voice tight. "Do you think Allastair knows we're working with Jack now? Or that Jack has his memory back?"

Jack responded, even though Nina's question wasn't necessarily for him. "I don't know. I mean, it's possible he'll think you found their jeweler by chance."

I snorted. "We told the guy we found him through you."

"Okay," Jack continued, "Well, even if he does make the connection between me and you, that doesn't mean he'll assume my memory is back. Maybe I told you about the guy last year. Who's to say? All the work that they put into what they did to me, they couldn't imagine you'd undo it as easily as you did. I've worked with this jeweler loads of times on projects totally unrelated to the Order. Maybe he'll just think it's a coincidence."

"Even though you didn't even remember us while you were brainwashed? How could we possibly be connected now if we weren't up to something?"

There was silence on the other end. "Jack? Seriously? Are you going to fix this?" There was more silence.

I should have cussed at Jack, told him to get his shit together and stop relying on his family for everything. I could have told him this was his fault for either being too stupid or too ignorant to realize the danger he'd just put us in. Because now, the Order knew we knew something. And that meant we were also a target.

But instead of throwing the fit I so wanted to, I hung up. My butt landed hard on the wooden bench as I sat down, my hands going to the sides of my head, cradling it.

"We didn't ask," I whispered to Nina, tears pricking my eyes in frustration. "We were stupid for not asking."

Nina's warm hand touched my leg. "I know. We should have. We shouldn't have blindly trusted Jack with something so important. He's an idiot, always has been."

"And so are we for not questioning him."

"We should all meet in private," Nina suggested. "See if Shalene will let us meet at her place again? Get everyone together to figure out our next move. I know you're pissed. So am I. But we need to figure something out, and fast."

I let my hands drop and leaned back in my seat. "You're right. I'll text Jack and tell him to meet us at Shalene's. We can figure out what to do then."

I slipped my phone from my pocket and asked Jack to meet us, as promised. My fingers hesitated over the messages screen, one final text needing to be sent as well. I pulled up Valentina's contact, the heart emoji I'd placed by her name making my heart skip a beat. I shot her a quick message, updating her on what happened, just in case.

SIXTEEN

There was a knock on the door. Without waiting for a response, Shalene's thin body slipped through the door, a designer handbag dangling on the crook of her elbow. "You guys are still here?"

"We're waiting for Jack," I replied, my lips pressed into a thin line. I sat on the edge of her bed, Nina laying on her back behind me, staring at the ceiling. Shalene snorted, the inelegant sound clashing with the rest of her vibe.

"It's been two hours. If he wanted to come, he would have."

I frowned. "It's a little more complicated than that." I tossed my phone around in my hand, running my thumb around its rectangular angles as I busied myself. Every so often I'd look down at the screen for a text, but there was nothing. Shalene was right, Jack bailed. He was probably scared of his family, and you know what? He should be. No amount of treasure can assure him his life. None of this was worth it, not really. But we needed him. I just hoped he'd pull through.

The sorority girl shrugged, tossing her hair over her shoulder in a way that reminded me of Valentina and made my heart hurt. She plopped into her vanity chair and pulled out a tray of lipsticks, choosing a nude shade and rubbing it all over her plump pout. "Look, I don't care if you guys want to hang around a bit more, but I have to get ready for a Delta Phi event. So if you need privacy, this isn't the place to have it."

I clicked the side of my phone and lit up my screen once more. The dozens of texts and calls to Jack remained unanswered, and Valentina still hadn't responded either. "I think we'll wait a bit longer." If Jack did show up, we'd need the cover of the sorority house to keep the Order off our trail. Not that we'd been doing a great job of that lately, but we had to at least try.

"Great," she replied brightly, "You can help me pick out my outfit. And Harper and I can chat about the ball."

I resisted a groan. "Awesome," I mumbled sarcastically, but Nina flipped onto her stomach at Shalene's offer to help her dress, her interest piqued.

Shalene stood and rummaged through her closet, pulling out a few cocktail dresses and handing them to Nina, who'd jumped up to help when Shalene had waved her over. The two of them chatted thoughtfully about colors and necklines, with Shalene's attention drifting back to me with questions every so often.

"So I heard Jack is no longer doing the debutante ball." Shalene slipped into a black mini dress with spaghetti straps and turned to look at her backside in the mirror.

I bit my lip. "You heard right." After shimmying the dress off and pulling on another, she turned to me.

"My sister isn't happy about that, you know."

I rolled my eyes. "He wasn't even her date. And our deal was for me, not for Jack."

Shalene ignored me for a few minutes as she assessed the various options she'd tried on, landing on the black dress she started with and slipping it back on. "Look, it's not that I care about Jack Cunningham. It's more that I'm worried about something else going wrong. If your plans for the ball are already falling apart, I'm concerned it will only get worse. The ball is in a matter of days, Harper. You realize that, right?"

I pressed my fingers to my temples. "Everything is fine, Shalene. Trust me, okay?" *I have bigger problems,* I thought, thinking to the woman and the rose pin.

Just as I was thinking that, Shalene sat down at her vanity again and opened up a drawer I hadn't noticed before. Nina idled by as she pulled out a large velvet box and opened it with a small delicate key. Rows and rows of expensive jewelry shined in my direction, everything from necklaces and earrings—all with various gemstones—to diamond rings and bracelets, including some with rubies, and there were plenty of them. Nina caught my eye, something pricking at her curiosity the same as it was mine.

"Um, Shalene?" Nina asked, ogling the jewels.

"Mm?" she replied, looking down as she placed a large pair of diamond earrings in her lobes.

"Do you know a lot about jewelry?" Nina asked.

"Does it look like I do?"

I stood up, something nagging at me. "Shalene, this may seem stupid, but have you ever seen a fancy rose pin made of diamonds and rubies? This would be a unique piece, not something you can just pick up at any store. I know it's a longshot, but—"

"Sure I have." The girl's attention was focused on locking her box and placing it back where it belonged, oblivious to the shock and urgency both Nina and I displayed.

"You...have?" I asked, staring at her face and hoping she'd look at me.

"Sure. It rings a bell. Did you lose it or something?"

"It wasn't mine," I managed to get out, and Shalene paused and looked up, thinking.

"Okay well now that I think about it, I mean, I remember seeing something like that years ago. At the debutante ball. You know, our year? Or, my year, I guess," she said, shooting a glance at me. "Can't remember who was wearing it though."

My heart sped up and I locked eyes with Nina, hope blossoming in my chest. "Are you serious? And you're sure you don't remember who was wearing it?"

She shook her head. "If you'd been there, maybe you'd have seen it."

My eyes darted back and forth as I thought this through. Whoever wore it must have been there for me. It's the only explanation. I was old enough to be separated from the Order at that point. Whoever had saved me from that tunnel had wanted to be there for my coming out. And they obviously felt it was safe enough to attend without catching the Orders' attention. What if that were the case this time around? If someone cared enough to come to my ball years ago, maybe they'd want that chance again. But how could I be sure they came? And how could I be sure they wore the pin so we could identify them?

I racked my brain. "There was a theme, wasn't there?"

This time, Shalene's full attention was on me, curious. "Well, there was a Parisian theme. But the reason everyone wore their best jewelry was because Tiffany's sponsored the ball and guests wanted to be sure to wear their best. All of us girls borrowed pieces from Tiffany's for the dance, which you'd know if you—"

"Okay! Shalene, that's enough. I'm sorry I bailed, okay? But I'm going this year. I'm *very much going*. Now, can we do something like that this year?"

She laughed. "My sister hasn't been very helpful cluing you in, has she? They decided not to do a theme this year. Just classic. And it's being sponsored by a mineral water company so no, no borrowed diamonds."

I gnawed on my bottom lip and started pacing. "Okay, but what if we switched to like, a jewel theme? All the guests could wear gem colors, and matching jewelry. In fact, the debs could all wear colors too. It could be a whole thing."

"You guys are supposed to wear white," Nina offered.

Shalene crossed her arms. "You want me to ask my mother to change the ball's theme days before the ball? New invites would have to be sent out. Invites that I am in charge of, by the way. Harper, that's ridiculous."

I sat down on the edge of the bed again, trying to look calm and rational, when inside, I was vibrating. "Okay, listen. You have to send out invites for me and

Edward anyway. And you don't have to send out *new* invites to everyone. Just add an amendment. The types of people going to this thing are rich enough to buy a new outfit at the last minute. And elite societies *love* to tell people what to do." I gripped my phone tighter in my hand, hoping my plea didn't come off too desperate. "Giving attendees restrictions just proves to them that this event is exclusive."

Shalene pursed her lips in thought.

"They'll like it, I promise." I urged. "And don't you think the debs want the chance to wear something *other* than white? Give me a break, that was an old school tradition anyway. Isn't the whole point of asking me to do this to make this year stand out?"

A wavy dark hair fell into Shalene's face and she brushed it behind her ear. "I don't know why, but this is clearly important to you, isn't it?"

I let out the breath I was holding, my eyes closing in dread. I knew this tone. It was the same one Shalene had when she bartered for my participation in this whole thing in the first place.

"What do you want?"

"If you want me to bend over backward to make this happen for you, Harper, you're going to need to get Jack back." A smug smile tugged at the corner of Shalene's lips. She was enjoying this. My throat constricted. For a dozen reasons, that would be a very big problem, if not impossible.

"Look, Shalene, I don't need Jack—"

"Not for you," she cut me off. "As my sister's date. That would change everything for her. Ultimately, that's the most important thing. Not what color the guests wear or what the theme is. If changing the theme to fit your needs would get Little S the man of her dreams, then I want you to make it happen, and I'll make my end happen."

"Can you do that?" Nina chirped.

I laughed, but there was no humor in it. "It's not much different from Newport, Nina. Over here there are certain families who run things too. Yes," I said, giving a tentative glance Shalene's way. "I think she could do it."

Shalene smiled broadly. "Okay then. You work on getting Jack as Little S's date. I'll work on my mother, and when she agrees, I'll amend the invites."

With Jack's name on them, I thought, taking a final glance at my empty phone screen, still no message from Jack. This was going to be a very big problem.

SEVENTEEN

It was comfortable, where I was. I was weightless, being supported by nothing but piles and piles of puffy dresses, their existence purely for my enjoyment and nothing else. But then I started slipping, my body sinking lower into the pile until everything went dark. I panicked, attempting to claw my way to the top, scratchy pieces of fabric pulling at my skin and slipping into my mouth as I tried to breathe.

The ball, I thought. I'm late for the ball. And somehow, these dresses know I'm not ready. They're punishing me, their jewel tones deceivingly beautiful. Not that I could see them anymore. I couldn't even see the hand in front of me. I was choking then, cloth and tulle blocking my airway, suffocating me until I tried to scream. The sound echoed around me as the dresses started falling away slowly until my head finally broke through the top of the pile, my vision returning to me. I sucked in a breath.

The dresses were no longer reflecting gorgeous colors, they were white. All of them. And they were wet. A metallic smell tickled my nose and I looked around, the dampness turning red, as if the Queen of Hearts had tossed a bucket of red paint on them. I screamed again, eager to get the red off me, to keep it from staining my skin.

"Harper!"

I shot up in bed, blinking hard. I struggled to bring my surroundings into focus, with only one dim light turned on on the far side of the room. My breath came out in bursts as I pushed my brain away from the events of my nightmare and into my bedroom, where Valentina was sitting on the edge of the bed, her hands resting on my blanket-covered thighs.

"V-Valentina?"

My skin tingled as she pulled me into a hug, her right hand rubbing my back as she held me. Tears sprung to my eyes. I wanted to tell her how empty it was when she left, to tell her everything that happened, and find out why she came back. But I couldn't grasp the words. Instead, a heavy sob wracked from my chest as I leaned into her, salty tears pouring down my face like it was the easiest thing in the world.

"I'm sorry," V said, her voice tight. I pulled away but kept my arms still partially around her. Tears pooled in V's own eyes. Her mouth was turned down into a pinched pout like she was holding something back.

"Why are you sorry?" I asked, thinking of her dad, and of the suffering she felt at the hands of her father's memory. She didn't have to be sorry. None of this was her fault.

She shook her head. "What do you mean, why am I sorry? I'm sorry for leaving you. I was being selfish. I felt...I felt guilty for what happened between our families. For what my dad did. I had to go home and tell Adan. He deserved to know. But it was stupid to just disappear and think you'd be fine. We don't do that stuff to each other. We just don't. I'm sorry."

She pulled me in again, crushing me against her. She smelled like detergent and vanilla. The chlorine smell that used to follow her around went away the minute we left Rhode Island, and I kind of missed it. My throat tensed as I tried to swallow a hard lump.

If this were last year, maybe I'd give her a hard time. I'd take it personally, her leaving. But things were different now. Valentina had proven so much to me since we'd gotten together, especially in these last few months when I needed her most. The last thing I planned to do was punish her when this was my chance to repay the favor. She needed me too now.

"We both have our own stuff," I said, my voice coming out weird against the pressure building in my sinuses. "I didn't blame you for leaving. I just...missed you. When you stopped responding that scared the hell out of me. I just wanted...I just want you to be okay."

"I just want *you* to be okay," she replied, her brow furrowing in earnest. "I was too wrapped up in everything to call. But I should have. I texted you a few hours ago when I left Rhode Island. I told you I was coming back. You didn't get it?"

My fingers reached automatically for my bedside where my phone was sitting. I clicked the button on the side to unlock my phone and noticed Valentina's name pop up on a few messages on the screen.

"No," I laughed, but the sound came out more like a snort. "I went to bed early." Of *course* I miss it the moment Valentina finally gets back to me. My face felt hot from crying, and even Valentina's face was red. "Thanks for letting me know."

I sighed, the weight of everything between V and me suddenly feeling far more complex than it had to be. "The whole point of this," I waved a hand between us, "is to take care of each other. We just have to remember that."

Valentina nodded and pressed her forehead to mine.

"So how did Adan take it?" I asked quietly, my eyes trained on her nose.

V's lips pressed together and she pulled away, looking down. "I don't know. He didn't really say anything. It seemed like he was thinking hard about something."

My brows furrowed. "He's still not talking to you?"

She glanced up at me. "Well, he did talk to me, actually."

"He did?"

"But only to tell me he'd only talk to you."

My heart skipped a beat. "What?

"He seemed like he might say something. For a second I really thought we'd have a breakthrough, like this new truth might have changed something. But instead, he said he needed to talk to you. It was important. He wouldn't tell me why." V swallowed hard. "And it must be, Harper. Because I'd just told our brother that his father, the man he was named after, was a murderer. And instead of comforting me or telling me we were in this together, that everything was going to be fine, he just said that there's something you need to know."

There's something you need to see. Dom's words from the night he died, almost eerily similar to Adan's, popped into my head. *There's something you need to know.* Could Adan know whatever it was Dom was trying to tell me? He'd found Dom. No one knows exactly what happened between them that day except that, thankfully, in the eyes of the law, Adan had not killed him. Was it possible he spoke to Dom before it happened? Or...or something else? And what did it have to do with his father?

I stared off into the distance, processing this. My train of thought was interrupted by Valentina's hand on my arm.

"I invited him to the debutante ball."

My chest seized. "V, you can't. Not with the danger we're in right now with the Order. He shouldn't even be coming to New York. You can't invite him."

Valentina held my gaze. "We're not going to win this one, Harper. Not if we continue making the same mistakes we made last time."

I closed my eyes. She was right. Valentina keeping Adan from the wedding was the reason he wasn't speaking to her now. And worse, it was the reason he was almost persecuted as a murderer.

"It doesn't matter though," she added. "He won't come. He won't leave Newport."

I shot to my feet. "But I can't go to Newport, V. Do you think Rebecca would just let me waltz back to town after everything she did to kick me out? I'd be making myself an even bigger target than I am now. At this point, the entire Cunningham family would know something was up. They'd probably just kill me. Can't I just call him?"

She shook her head. "He was very serious about wanting to tell you in person." *Just like Dom.* Her lips formed a thin line. "Which is also why I'm certain this is big."

I fell back onto the bed, staring at the ceiling, and V joined me. "We'll figure something out," she offered. "Eventually. We need to know what Adan knows. But from what I hear, we have a more urgent situation to worry about."

"So you did read my messages."

"And got on a train over here as quickly as I could. I'm sorry. Again." V turned her head to look at me. "So you have a plan?"

"It's in motion. But we have a huge problem." I let out a breath. "Jack disappeared."

"You think when the Order busted our lead he freaked out and left?"

My bare toes tapped the cold floor rhythmically as I spoke. "He must have. If he's been made, they'd definitely kill him this time. I don't really blame him. It's not safe for him. Problem is, we need him for the debutante ball. And to outsmart his family."

V bit her lip. "He must have gone to his family in Japan."

"The Matsudas," I whispered, thinking of the painting of his father, who we'd learned had made Allastair Cunningham's list of Order-related deaths. "They're a powerful family. And they must blame the Order for what they did to Jack's dad. I bet they'd be able to protect him. Smart."

"Mm," she agreed. "But are you sure he's gone?"

My shoulders touched my ears and I raised them in a shrug. "Unless they already found him and killed him." That terrifying thought occurred to me and sent fear through my body. "Unless he spoke to the jeweler himself and stole our lead. Maybe he was playing dumb the other day. For all we know he already found the woman with the rose pin. He could be in New York still and we'd never know for sure. It's not like we can just burst into his fraternity and check."

V nudged me with her elbow. "Why not? If he's really gone, so are his guard dogs."

I sat up, my long hair bouncing against my back.

"Yeah, you're right. Why not?"

And that was the very energy I kept as I burst through the wooden door to Jack's bedroom in the Phi Gamma house the next day, Valentina by my side. Of course, someone had let us in the front door, but that didn't make our entrance any less aggressive. I imagined wood splintering and the lock breaking as my booted foot met the cork door, whereas in reality, it hadn't even been locked to begin with.

Still, the surprised scream that we got as soon as we burst in made the entire thing all the more satisfying.

"Jack?" Valentina said, her eyes landing on the cowering freshman sitting in a desk chair with his hands covering his face. Slowly, his hands fell, and when he saw who was standing in his doorway, his face soured.

"Oh, what are you two doing here?" he asked, though he didn't really sound like he wanted to know.

My mouth dropped open. "Jack?!" I walked quickly to where he was sitting and grabbed his dress shirt in my hands.

The royal pain in my ass rolled his eyes and shrugged me off. "Well who else were you expecting?"

he monotoned, whirling back around to his open laptop to continue typing.

"You've been here the whole time?" I yelled, spinning his chair back around.

Jack scoffed and stood up, puttering around the room as if he was fixing it up, when really the space was already pristine. "Where else would I be?"

"Jack, you disappeared. We couldn't get in touch with you. We thought the Order killed you. Or that you took off." With that, my eyes drifted to a set of matching luggage nestled by the closet. By the looks of it, it was full.

"Going somewhere, Jack?" I asked, pointing to the incriminating evidence.

Jack shrugged. "Just getting ready for a quick exit. When we've found our woman, that is. And to answer your earlier question, I wasn't ignoring you. I got a new phone. It's called laying low." *Bullshit,* I thought. Jack stepped in front of the luggage, as if blocking it from our view would end the conversation. He jutted a chin at Valentina. "You went radio silent too."

Valentina stalked over to him and grabbed him by the collar, dragging him to his twin bed and forcing him to sit down. "And how are we supposed to find the rose pin woman, Cunningham? Do you even know about our new plan? No. Because you ran scared. We need to stick together more than ever." V looked out the window. "And did it occur to you that getting a new phone makes you look even more suspicious? What did your guard dogs think?"

Jack narrowed his eyes. "What did they think of you bursting in here?" Valentina's face fell, and so did mine. For some reason, neither V nor I actually expected Jack would be here. Valentina let go of Jack's collar and we both jogged to the window, peering out at the busy street with cars lined on either side. I pointed to a black van at one end.

"Shit," I muttered. "That looks like their van. We walked right by it."

"Wait," Valentina said. "Right there." She pointed to two men walking slowly down the sidewalk with paper cups in their hands. "They must have gone for coffee or were doing their rounds or something. I think we're good." We let out a collective sigh. After all the work we'd put in to avoid being caught with

Jack, I was going to be pissed if we got caught right in the clutch. And something told me they would be, too.

"Good," Jack said, anger dripping from his voice. "You two are putting me in a lot of danger by being here."

I threw my hands up. "You put us in a lot of danger, asshole! Sending us right to an Order connection with precious information? Are you stupid?"

My phone beeped, and I looked down at it automatically, pulling it from my pocket. The message was from Shalene, asking if I'd secured Jack as Little S's date. I closed my eyes, groaning.

"Seems like I'm not your only problem," Jack muttered, crossing his arms in interest.

"Oh how I wish you were," I mumbled.

I texted Shalene back.

Got him. Jack is on board. Good to go.

I didn't know if I was going to eat my words with that text, but I tried to push the thought away as a new text came in.

Good. Jewel theme is secured. Digital invites going out in a few hours.

Perfect, I thought. I'd have to sneak into Shalene's bedroom after we finished with Jack and remove his name from the new invites she was sending out, just as a precaution. I didn't know how we were going to solve the problem of the Order finding out about Jack. Maybe we'd just have him bail on Little S. By then it would be too late, and at least I'd have held up part of my end of the bargain. But one thing was for sure—Jack would need to be there, on-site, out of view, but nearby. If this mystery woman came through for us with information, there was a good chance we'd need Jack's inside scoop into the Cunningham family and the Order. He might know what to do to take them down.

Plus, we were going to need him to use his family connections in Japan to give the woman a safe haven, in case the Order found out about her. We'd fly her out of New York tomorrow if we had to. Whatever it took to find her and keep her safe, along with whatever information she could tell us. We just needed Jack along for the ride.

"You can have all the money," I said, my eyes trained on Jack. "I don't care. But you have to help us with the ball. You have to help us find this woman. Especially if your grandfather is looking for her now, we need to find her first. She's our only chance."

I didn't want the money. It's not like I needed it. But more than anything, I'd seen what money could do. I saw what it did to my mom, whose entire world for many years was maintaining her socialite status after the divorce. I saw what it did to Macy, who was only marrying my dad for the very same reason. And then there was Dom. We all saw what it did to Dom, and he didn't even have any wealth of his own. But it was *because* of money that all of this happened in the first place—to find the treasure, to keep it a secret, to use its power. I didn't want any of that. I just wanted to take down the Order.

A smile played on one corner of Jack's lips. "All the treasure? Everything Malloy had?"

"All of it. Of course, our original deal still stands. We take down the Order together. That might require the use of some of that money, but I'm sure getting rid of your biggest threat is what you want anyway. We take them down, and then you can do whatever you want with the rest after."

He stared at me for a long moment. "I'm going to need to hear this plan. If it's good, and if I'm assured that I can leave for Japan right away after we find this woman, before my grandfather or his flunkies can find me, I'll do it. I need to be assured of my safety."

I nodded. "It is good. You can, and you will. We just need you for one more day. Just one, Jack." I held up my pointer finger. "Can you do that?"

After a moment, he nodded.

I stepped into the threshold of his doorway and peered out. "Is Edward here?"

A beefy frat boy walking by me stopped at my question, even though I hadn't been asking him. "Huh? Oh, yeah. Edward! Come here man."

The guy Jack had chosen as my new debutante date strolled into the hallway, eyebrows raised. "Yeah? Oh. Hey."

I smiled a half smile. "Valentina, meet my date for the ball. He can help us keep tabs on Jack, just to be sure he actually shows up." Valentina nodded and walked into the hallway, looping one arm through Edward's and dragging him back into his room.

"Sounds good," she replied, giving me a wink. The door shut behind them, and whether she planned to bribe him or scare him into helping us, I wasn't sure.

I turned back to Jack, still holding my phone, pulled up my social media, and crafted a quick post.

I'm pleased to announce I'll be coming out at the New York Debutante Ball tomorrow evening. To all my friends and family, hope to see you there!

And then, cringing, but knowing I couldn't afford subtlety here, I added *Wear your best jewels, I know I will!*

I hit post, exposing my commitment to this charade to the entire world. Well, to all of my followers, at least. That included Rebecca, and probably plenty of other spies for the Order. It also included, I hoped, the woman with the rose pin. I was sure my mom had already spread the word of my participation in this thing to everyone who knew me, but I had to be sure.

With that, I locked eyes with Jack. "Alright. Now, let's talk about this plan. This year, we'll have a lot more to worry about than a lopsided curtsy."

EIGHTEEN

We were early, but even still guests lingered outside the hotel doors dressed in their best. Valentina, Nina and I pushed by them in our casual clothes, careful not to step on anyone's dress skirts, and made our way inside.

"I wish Jack could just come with us now so we could keep an eye on him," Valentina grumbled, her words echoing through the lobby. A dainty hand went to the thick, cropped hair grazing her shoulder and tucked it behind her ear.

Nina wrung her hands together. "You think he won't?" There was an edge to her voice as she clung to V's arm.

"His bags were packed. He was planning on bailing. I don't blame him, but I just hope we gave him enough motive to stick around this time. Still, if he just came *with* us…"

I lowered my voice so only my group could hear me. "You know we can't risk Jack being seen. By anyone, but least of all Little S. This plan is only going to work if he's here, but you know…out of sight."

"And if we find the woman with the pin, we can hide her in the room we booked with cash last night, where Jack will be. Find out what she knows. And then…?" Nina asked, stopping in the middle of the lobby, the clicking sound of her shoes going silent.

I stopped too, and huddled close. "And then we let Jack take her to Japan. Or we all go, if it comes to it, to keep her and us safe. If she wants, I mean. By finding her we're putting her in a lot of danger. She can't just leave and go about her business. Our end goal is to get her and all of us out safely and get whatever information we can from her."

"If we find her," Valentina pointed out, her arms crossed. I shot her a look. "What? It's true. There's a reasonable chance she won't even come to this. What if she's dead? What if the Order took our lead and already found her? Did anyone think of that? Or like, what if she's in Europe or something?"

Nina gave me a panicked look.

"Okay, V, that's enough. You're scaring Nina. The Order knows we're up to something, yes. But if they're waiting to make a move, it's because they *need* something. Or maybe they want more information first. They must not have her, and may not even know who it is we're looking for. And look, sure, she might not come. But we have to operate on the chance that she *might*. That's literally all we can do, okay?"

Nina wrung her hands together. "But, Harper, what happens to Jack if the lady with the pin doesn't show up? We didn't talk about that." *What happens to us,* I wondered silently. I thought about the brainwashing the Order so easily achieved on Jack, and how likely it would be that we'd be next if we failed.

I frowned, my eyes fixed on the massive chandelier dangling from the ceiling. "We let him go."

"What?" V hissed, and I slid my arm through hers and Nina's, moving them along. We continued walking, but I could tell they were expecting an answer from me.

"We're not like the Order, we're not monsters. Jack can't just stay here. If this doesn't work, he should leave, to protect himself. He's taking the biggest risk."

"Goddamnit," V cursed. "Then let's hope she really is here today."

The hotel was bustling with guests dressed in rich, vibrant colors. Some were visitors from out of town, possibly from different countries, all drawn to the pull of the exclusive event. I was overcome with a rush of adrenaline as I stepped into the small room connected to the ballroom. Because, of course, a fancy hotel such as this would have a backstage area built in.

The male dates must have been getting ready across the hall, because this too-cramped space was filled with young women and some of their mothers, racks of newly purchased clothes, perfume and makeup clouding every inch of space. The entire scene reminded me that this was still, in fact, a performance. My stomach dropped. I felt Valentina slide her hands in mine.

"Okay, let's get changed," she whispered, her eyes scanning the room for a place to change. A few of the mothers cut glances our way, possibly irritated and on to the fact that their last-minute dress purchases were a result of my doing. That, or the space was already too tight and two more additions were two too many. Still, some of the girls gave me soft smiles, and I wondered how many of them were grateful to branch out into more interesting, vibrant looks instead of the stuffy white gowns that all looked the same.

Many of the girls were already dressed, with plunging necklines that dipped just enough. Some wore strapless dresses and others halter necks, some with thick straps and some with thin. Some gowns had tulle and some fit tightly against the wearer's curves, each look bringing something fresh to the ball. It was much more than the range of color that changed the entire vibe of this event. Instead of looking like virginal brides, the girls looked more like what I would expect them to look like at prom.

"I'm going to stand watch out here," Nina whispered to us in the doorway. "Let me know when you're ready and I'll go get dressed. Someone should really keep eyes on this ball the whole time." V and I nodded, waving to her as she closed the door behind us.

We found a corner behind a rack and quickly pulled off our clothes, sliding our dresses out from the garment bags we'd had the doorman deliver back here this morning. Part of me wondered if Little S would take the opportunity to cut my gown to pieces, but the chances of her sabotaging me now, after promising her Jack as her date, were minimal. *Just wait until she finds out he isn't going to show,* I thought.

My breathing was quick. I focused hard on the satin of my amethyst-colored dress slipping between my fingers as I stepped my feet inside. The material caressed my body as it slid up my skin, this dress-choice proving far more comfortable than anything my mother could have picked out for me. I felt my girlfriend's hands go to my zipper, her finger pulling the sides taut as she pulled the metal piece up my back, closing it just a little too tight. The gesture made me smile, reminding me of one of our first real interactions on the beach the night of the Order recruitment.

This time, I'd chosen purple. I wouldn't dare to stand out with something bright like pink, or too eye-catching like red. Purple stood for power, ambition, mystery—all things I hoped to find within myself at this ball. The dress suited me the way I hoped it would, bringing me just enough attention to play the part, but not so much that I couldn't float into the background when I needed to. Though I didn't see Little S yet, I was sure her gem choice would be something overpowering.

I looked over my shoulder at V with a coy smile, but my expression dropped immediately at the sight of my girlfriend. Valentina stood before me in a jet-black dress, also made of some kind of silky material, the entire gown cascading down her frame like it had been custom made for the Met Gala.

V's lips pinched together. "You don't like it?"

I let out a laugh, my smile pushing right back up my cheeks. "No, of course I love it. I was just surprised. It's like, no matter how long we're together, your beauty never gets old." I slapped my hand to my forehead. "Ugh, sorry, that was so cheesy. I don't mean to sound like that, but…" I sighed. "You're the first person who has ever made me *want* to say cheesy things and mean it. They just slip out of my mouth sometimes."

A blush spread across Valentina's cheeks. She held my hand and let her forehead drop onto mine. "I feel the same way. You're beautiful, and someone should really tell you. Spoiler alert, it's going to be me."

I almost leaned in to kiss her, but something nagged at me. V frowned.

"Sorry, let's talk in the hall and let Nina get changed." I cleared my throat. Suddenly the pressing of people in this room felt too much. A memory swarmed my brain of the last time I did this, of what happened. Kissing V here, now, felt like the most right thing in the world and somehow also wrong. I hated to think of me and V like that.

"Sure," Valentina said quietly, probably confused at my pulling back. "But wait. You're going to need these." In one hand was a pair of heels and in the other was my cell phone.

"Oh right, duh. Sorry, I'm kind of scattered right now." I took the phone from her hand and took the garters Valentina had procured for us, pulled mine up my leg and shoved my cell phone in the handy little pocket that came attached. You could buy anything online these days. After slipping my shoes on I headed toward the door with V following behind me. We wandered into the hallway, finding Nina at one of many entrances to the ballroom.

"I haven't heard from Jack at all," Nina said before we had a chance to speak. "That Edward guy isn't answering his texts either. I even checked the room we're supposed to meet in later when we find pin lady. Nothing. Jack isn't here."

A pit formed in my stomach. "He must just be late, that's all. He's supposed to be. He has to ditch his guards and slip in. He'll be here," I choked out.

Nina stuck her hand against a heavy champagne curtain hanging in the archway, pulling away the fabric to reveal a sliver of the now bustling ballroom. There was a wide empty space in front of the stairs leading up to the second floor. The sight of it formed an even larger knot in my stomach. It wouldn't be long before we'd be expected to line up on those stairs, each taking a turn being introduced to the world as *young ladies*. And before that, even, we'd be expected to dance on that very floor, just as we rehearsed.

"We have a problem." Nina's voice was tight. She pointed past the elegant circle tables filling the room beyond the dance floor to a crowd mingling in the back of the room. At first I didn't see who she was talking about, because there were loads of guests taking the opportunity to socialize before we got started. And then I saw it.

"Rebecca," I breathed, a chill running up my spine. "Oh no."

"Yes," Nina squeaked. "I'm starting to wonder if Jack saw her and bolted."

I swallowed hard, my voice coming out in a whisper. "I wouldn't blame him if he did."

"Okay, no," V interjected, her hands going to my shoulders and redirecting my attention. "We're not going to freak out here. We're not going to let what happened last time cloud our judgment. We don't need Jack. We just have to avoid Rebecca at all costs. She's probably here because she thought Jack would be. If he's not here, we can play it off, and pretend this is exactly what it is. Just a ball."

Nina let the curtain drop. "And if we find the woman? How are we going to get her out of here without Rebecca seeing if we don't have the private jet Jack promised us?"

Valentina bit her bottom lip. "Well, this is a huge hotel. And we're in New York, for God's sake. No one knows it like Harper. We just need to find a way to sneak her out and get her somewhere far away from here. Jack isn't the only one with a private jet. We'll just have to deal with our exit plan later."

"Right," I agreed halfheartedly.

"Now Nina, you go get changed," V said. "Harper and I will keep our eye for any guests wearing the pin, and for Jack."

I grabbed Nina's arm as she turned. "Just hurry up though, the dance starts soon. And we need to find Edward so Shalene doesn't roast me for doing the entire dance by myself. I'm already in hot water if Jack doesn't materialize for Little S."

V pulled the curtain to the side again, just enough so that we could see in but no one could see us. We stood there together in silence after Nina left, taking in the reality of our situation. My hands dropped to my sides, running over imaginary pockets for something, anything to fiddle with, until I realized I had nothing on me except my phone. Valentina must have noticed, because she grabbed my roaming hand and held it firmly by her side. The sound of live instruments began playing from somewhere on the second floor, violins and flutes and other elegant instruments finding the right note before we began.

A quiet "*Oh, god*" slipped from my mouth before I could stop myself. V turned to look at me.

"Oh come on," Valentina said, attempting to sound playful, but the strain in her voice giving her away. "You must have seen worse than this. I mean, something must have happened last time around that was bad enough to make you quit. You didn't even have a murderous elite organization hunting you down." She threw in that last part with an edge to her voice, her eyes pointed at Rebecca.

I shook my head. "No, just a few homophobic adults stuck on their straight agenda."

V's head turned in my direction, her brows coming together.

"There was a girl," I started, and V lowered her hand from the curtain, her attention now only on me.

"This is weird." I added, hesitating.

"No, tell me. It's not weird. I want to know what happened."

I stared at my black strappy heels. "Well, like I said, there was this girl. She was coming out too. As a woman, I mean, at the ball. We clicked instantly. We wanted to go together, to be each other's dates. I kept pushing for it, and the ladies in charge that year kept pretending they were going to let us. They had male dates picked out just to 'practice the dance, just for now'." I put air quotes around that last part. "Sure, the guy would have to present us, but at least we could do the dance together. I should have known. Looking back it was so obvious. But at the time I was hopeful." Valentina reached for me, and I took her hand.

"So when I showed up at the ball, gown and all—"

"You showed up?"

"Yes, I showed up. No one really knows that though because when I got there one of the moms in charge told me I wasn't going to be able to dance with the girl after all. She said it wasn't how things were done. They tricked me to get me there. It wasn't even about my date anymore; it was bigger than that. So I left, before anyone else saw me."

V closed her eyes at the conclusion of my story, my hesitation at doing this ball in the first place and my distance when she tried to kiss me earlier finally making sense to her. "Oh, Harper."

"I already felt like I wasn't myself doing this kind of thing. I only did it because of my crush…and maybe a little bit for my mom. But when it became clear that they didn't want any single part of me at that ball, I made their wish come true."

My leg vibrated, and I jumped a little. "Nina just texted," I realized, pulling my phone from my leg garter and swiping quickly. I ignored the messages from my mom and the surprised social media replies my post from last night had gotten, only to all but panic when Nina's message cropped up on my screen.

Guess who I just found in our hotel room? We have a big problem.

Another text came through.

Sorry, I know I said that before already. But now we really do.

I held the phone close to my face as an image popped up on the screen. Valentina leaned her body close to mine to see it. We both gasped. A photo of Edward appeared on the screen, his feet tied together and his wrists tied to the metal rod in the empty bathtub he was in. His mouth was covered in duct tape, and his designer suit was covered in wrinkles. Which, all things considered, was the least of his problems.

"That little shit!" Valentina shouted. "That's the rope we tied Jack up with." Her hands flew to her head in frustration. "Look at that crappy ropework, that's definitely Jack!"

"Crappy? Yes. But it worked well enough on Edward. Looks like he came through and got Jack here. He just couldn't keep him here."

Nina texted again.

Jack is def gone. Look.

Another photo came through, this time of a slightly crumpled piece of hotel stationary. I zoomed in on the handwritten scribbles, groaning as I scanned the message.

Sorry, H. It's not worth the risk. You're smart, I'll give you that. You just might make it out of here alive. But I won't, not with my family on my every move. This is my one chance to leave, with everyone occupied by the ball. I had to take it. If you get what you need, you know where to find me. Best of luck.

"Shit," I cursed, looking at Valentina. "He went to the Matsudas."

"They *will* definitely protect him," she added, shaking her head. "Could have seen this coming."

I glanced back at the photo of the letter and read the last line.

P.S. Please ingest this message. All evidence of my treachery must be destroyed.

My phone vibrated again as Nina sent something else.

I'm not eating this, by the way. In fact, I kind of want to hold onto it, just in case...But I'll shove it down the shower drain or something. He sounds sorry.

He did sound sorry. And the truth was, Jack may be a pompous asshole, but he's gone through way more than any one person should have to. We all have. But this *was* his chance to get away from it. I wished I didn't understand, but I did.

Thanks, I texted back, not having any more time to mull over Jack's intentions. *Just start untying Edward ASAP. It's crunch time.*

Another vibration.

That's going to take me a few minutes. Stay tuned.

I let my hand drop, my phone heavy in my palm. So much for the alliance with Jack, I thought. Music swelled above us, so loud I would have jumped if my body wasn't so in tune with the familiar melody by now.

"Oh no," I whispered. "We don't have a few minutes. There's no way Edward is going to get down here in time, even with Nina's help."

My fingers flew across my phone's keypad in a matter of seconds.

Okay but hurry, we're starting, which means the woman with the pin should be here soon if she isn't already. We don't want Rebecca to spot her first.

After I hit *send,* V and I stuck our heads through the curtain to assess the situation. The guests were seated and the lights were now dimmed. A low chatter spread throughout the room in anticipation. The dance was starting. "Forget Edward, the entrance is on the other side of the ballroom anyway. I'm fucked."

The sound of dozens of high heels clacked across the tile as young ladies and their dates descended onto the dance floor. What looked almost like a perfect rainbow glimmered across from me, the mix of vivid blues, greens, reds and every jewel tone you could imagine meshing together to create an accidental symbol of the gayness I wasn't allowed to show last time around. A chill prickled up my spine as I realized that this time, intentionally or not, I had broken all the rules and brought a little piece of myself to the girls in front of me. No more hiding.

And yet somehow, I was standing on the sidelines once again. "Every single thing that could go wrong today, has," I said, my voice shaking.

"Not this." Valentina's gloved hand grabbed gently at my arm, pulling me through the curtain.

"What are you doing?" I protested, feeling a few eyes on me as we entered the dance floor from the wrong end of the room.

"Giving you that dance you always wanted," Valentina answered, stopping us right in the front of the group where Little S should have been, but wasn't. I silently appreciated how easily I'd avoided a confrontation with her up to this point, realizing everything would, without a doubt, go to hell after this dance. I might as well enjoy it.

"And look," V whispered, assuming the position both Edward and Jack had when they led me through this dance each time. "I'm even wearing black just like all the gentlemen here."

The music swelled again, cuing the ladies to curtsy, and our dates to bow. I watched in awe as Valentina performed each move with precision as we moved around the dance floor, spinning me with ease, dipping me when necessary, and leading like she was born for it. Maybe she was. Her height had certainly helped. Thank God for that, because with our position in the group, and in all likelihood, our uncommon pairing, all eyes were on us.

"What gem is black, anyway?" I asked amid our hundredth curtsy and dip of the night. My cheeks hurt, and I realized I'd been smiling the entire time. There was something so inherently different about doing this waltz with someone I actually wanted to be holding me up and moving me across the room. It felt right in a way nothing had in a long time. I knew I should have been taking the moment to scan the room for the rose pin, or even keep my eye on Rebecca. But I couldn't.

Amidst all the chaos that was today, I allowed myself the thrill that was dancing with Valentina Vasquez.

V pulled me in close, one hand on my lower back. "Onyx," she whispered, answering my question. With one final crescendo of violins we took our final positions, ending in a very deep, and very uncomfortable, curtsy-and-bow combination made worse by the complex positioning of Valentina's arms. Even still, she'd nailed it just right.

"You learned all that from watching?" I asked her as we shuffled gracefully off of the dance floor, hand-in-hand alongside the other debutantes, creating what I imagined would look like a kaleidoscope from above. When we crossed behind the curtain to the hallway it instantly filled with chatter, the girls and guys in a fluster of excitement from the performance. Even I was caught up in the moment, until I ran smack dab into my second worst enemy of the day. Little S. Although seeing the look on her face, I suddenly wasn't sure who I was more scared of—her, or the Order of the Six.

NINETEEN

Valentina took a protective step in front of me as the rest of the group scattered down the hallway and out of sight, though their gossiping lingered audibly in the background. V must have seen what I'd seen. Squinty, accusing eyes, clenched fists probably hiding perfectly manicured talons, and vicious snarl on Little S's perfectly powdered face. Or at least, that's what you'd see if you could peer through the layers of perfectly powdered makeup and delicate pink fabric encasing her body.

"Harper Fontaine," she started, taking a step toward us. Her baby pink dress and matching pearls shimmered as she moved, creating an unfitting contrast to the menacing girl in front of us. Valentina and I took an automatic step back in tandem, looking almost like we were still dancing.

I jumped in, hoping to cut off Little S's tantrum before it started. "I'm so sorry, Shyla. I did everything I could to get Jack here. He was supposed to be here."

"He was," Valentina added, her eagerness to quell Little S not giving me much confidence. If the most revered girl at Wellesley Prep was nervous, I certainly should be.

The seething debutante took another step in our direction.

"Just hear me out—" I started, but was interrupted by a fourth voice growing louder behind me.

"What the hell was that Harper?" Shalene's exasperated voice was directed at me. Then, she turned to her sister. And where were you?"

"My date didn't show up," Little S snarled, her eyes still on me.

"My date got caught up," I added.

Shalene threw her hands up. The sheen of her emerald-green dress and matching emerald jewelry reflected in the light as she moved. "Are you serious? One missing date I can explain, but now two?"

"If Jack wasn't on the invitations, no one should even know he's missing but us though, right?" I reasoned, grateful I'd successfully intervened in that department, just as I'd planned.

Shalene put her hands on her hips. "He *was* on the invitations Harper. I sent out new ones, remember?" My heart thudded. "I almost sent them out without double-checking, but I'm nothing if not thorough. I must have forgotten to save the updated versions, because when I checked, Jack's name wasn't on them."

Air seeped out of my lungs. Valentina's hand went to mine and squeezed. "But you added him back on. And sent them to everyone," she said quietly.

"Including his family," I said in a low breath. Oh no. That explains Rebecca's presence. I mean, I wouldn't put it past her to find out anyway, but having Jack's name on the invitations, invitations that also listed *my* name as a debutante would have shot up a thousand red flags to the Cunninghams. I thought I fixed it by hacking Shalene's computer late last night. I was wrong.

"Who cares!" Little S yelled. "Forget his family, what about me?"

"You know what? I'm surprised it was him that bailed," Shalene interjected. "You're the one that's been missing all morning, Harper. A bunch of people said they saw you, and then you just disappeared."

I fought the urge to roll my eyes and took a step out from behind Valentina. "I wasn't missing, I just…was looking for my date Edward, I couldn't find him and then mixed up the entrance. I was trying to get everything sorted before we got started." It was a half-lie, but I'd run with it.

"Well I didn't have a date either, and somehow *I* missed the entire dance! You know why? Because it's *always* about Harper Fontaine. You'll do anything for the spotlight, won't you? I won't let you have it." Little S stuck a hand out and shoved one side of my shoulder hard, forcing me to stumble backward.

"Oh no you don't," Valentina threatened, and without missing a beat, used both her hands to shove Little S backward. When she stumbled, Shalene's mouth dropped open.

"Okay! That's enough! We aren't doing this here!"

But Little S missed the memo, because she didn't hesitate before wrapping her bony fingers around Valentina's thick silky hair and pulling as hard as she could. Little S may have been an average sized girl, but she was ruthless. I rushed over, my hands going over my girlfriend's in an attempt to help her rip her attacker's hands from her hair.

When she didn't budge, a flare of anger burst through me. Absolutely *not*. I would *not* let some snooty girl harass my girlfriend, the only person who has made the day bearable, to get back at me. With Little S distracted, I jumped on her back, my arms circling her neck, compelling the teenager to let my girlfriend go. Two things happened in that moment. First, Little S and I flew backward, her grip on Valentina's shiny hair no longer keeping her in place. We, or more accurately, I, smacked my back hard into the wall behind us, the two of us separating and falling to the floor.

Second, Valentina flew back as well, but instead of a wall breaking her fall, it was Shalene. The girls also ended up with their backs to the floor, and the lot of us looked like we'd just been trampled by elephants.

"That's it!" Shalene yelled, grabbing at her dress skirt and tripping a little as she pulled herself off the ground. "My mother will be back here any second, and she can deal with this mess! I should have never asked you to do this Harper, you're only good at one thing, and that's ruining everything!"

A vibration shot up my leg. Nina. The sensation reminded me that I had a job to do. I couldn't get kicked out of the ball yet, or I'd never find the woman with the pin, much less step out into the ballroom to look. I had to fix this, now.

Still on the floor, I pulled my phone from my garter as V and Little S collected themselves, the tension in the room so thick it felt like anyone could snap at any moment.

Edward is leaving! I don't blame him though, should I let him?

"Shit," I muttered incoherently.

No, I'll go get him. Change of plans. We need him to be Little S's date. V will keep an eye out for the rose pin.

V helped me up, looking over my shoulder as Nina's latest text popped up.

K. He's heading to the lobby. I'll meet you.

"Go," V whispered. "I'll look for our mystery guest in the ballroom from the second floor."

I turned to face Little S, who was shoving a foot back into a cream-colored pump five inches high. "I'm going to get Edward for you. He was supposed to be my date, but he can be yours. Let him present you. I'm sorry I made you miss the dance. Let me fix it."

She looked like she was about to protest, her lips quivering in anger, but Shalene put a hand on her sister's arm.

I shuffled over to the elevator, pressing the button and watching the doors open. Before I stepped in I looked over my shoulder. "And Shalene," I said, getting her attention. "I did what you asked. I showed up. And before you drag me to Mrs. P, remember you got the other thing you wanted." I took a step into the elevator. "This ball will definitely be a night no one forgets."

TWENTY

Ding. The elevator chimed when I finally hit the floor labeled "L", its door sliding open into the lobby.

"Please still be here, please be here," I said to myself, scanning the large, bustling space for my runaway date.

"Gotcha." I spotted Edward hustling to the spinning doors at the front entrance, his coat slipped-off and dangling from his arm, collar popped and tie undone. My fingers sunk into the slippery material of my dress as I pulled it up, running after him.

"Edward!" I yelled. He must not have heard me over the rest of the mindless chatter around us, so I yelled his name again, this time grabbing his elbow as I reached him.

The poor guy yanked his arm away from me instinctually, turning to see who'd grabbed him. He relaxed when he realized it was me.

"Leave me alone," he said. "I'm out of here."

"Wait, wait, wait!" I stepped in front of him, holding my hand up just inches from his chest. "Please don't go yet. I'm sure we can make it worth your while. You wouldn't even be my date anymore, you'd be Little S's."

Edward crossed his arms, unconvinced. "Yeah right. After what Jack did to me? The lot of you conned me into doing this just so I could end up tied up in an empty hotel room. Forget it." He stepped to the side, and I mirrored his movement, cutting him off.

"What did they promise you?" I asked. "Valentina, or Jack. Whoever had you agreeing to this in the first place. You must have done it for a reason. What was it? Money? We can give you more."

He scoffed. "Do I look like I need money?"

I shook my head. "Okay, then what do you want? Everyone has a price."

I watched as he crossed his arms and assessed me, looking me up and down. After a moment, his glance darted around him, as if he was going to say something he didn't want others to hear. I waved him into a quiet corner of the lobby, tucked away with a water fountain and a great view of the rest of the room.

"I want Jack gone," he demanded, his mouth pressed into a scowl. "I was doing him a solid because I thought it would get me in good with the rest of the frat, but he's just making me look bad. I want him out."

"Out of the fraternity?"

"Sure. Or out of the country, I don't care. Just get the guy away from me and I'll be someone's date."

My lips quirked up into a smile. Jack was already gone. And even if he wasn't, our plan had always been for Jack to leave after we found our woman. Finally, something worked out perfectly on this terribly chaotic day.

The sound of high heels clicking rapidly against the floor grew louder as Nina appeared behind Edward. "Is he staying? Are you staying?" she asked, looking from me to Edward.

I raised my eyebrows and locked eyes with Nina. "Yes. Edward is going to stay if we get rid of Jack."

Nina's lips turned down. She stepped next to Edward. "But he's—"

"Definitely not going to bother Edward anymore," I said slowly, tipping my head down as I spoke, hoping she'd pick up on my meaning. People continued traversing behind them, a reminder that every second I wasted here was another moment the lady with the rose pin could be wandering around the ballroom in Rebecca's grasp. The introductions would start soon, and at the very least, Edward had to be there.

My friend looked between Edward and me. "Oh, right, yeah, we'll totally be sure to handle Jack for you. Like, you don't even have to worry about it, he's *sooo* finished." The rest of her words filtered into the background as I spotted something familiar on the other end of the lobby. At first, my mind didn't register what it was, just that somewhere in the back of my mind, I knew I should be focusing my attention over there. And then I saw it—the flash of the chandelier reflecting down on a piece of fine jewelry, standing out against a woman's milky white gown.

The world slowed. Red on white. Blood, on a wedding gown. I saw it then, Valentina's mother crouched by Dom, his blood staining fabric. But no, Miss Vasquez had never done that. My head swam. This wasn't the wedding. The woman wasn't Miss Vasquez. And the glint of red I'd seen hadn't been blood. It had been the rose pin.

I squinted and pushed between Nina and Edward in front of me, desperate to get a closer look. I spun around, spotting the elevator the woman had been heading toward. There was a crowd waiting patiently for a ride, both elevators making their way slowly from the top floors. But the woman in the white dress wasn't there. My eyes shot around nearby until a flash of white caught my eye, illuminating the shadowed hallway of the stairwell.

The stairs, I thought. *She's taking the stairs. I have to stop her.* My feet moved me in her direction automatically, but something pulled me backward.

"Harper?" Nina's arm rested in the crook of my elbow. I blinked.

"I'm going to look for someone." My words tumbled out in a rush. "Get Edward to Little S. I'll text you." Nina's eyes grew big and round, but she let me go. I didn't look back as I walked as quickly as I could to the staircase.

The doorway to the stairs opened with a heavy squeak, the partially dim area looking a confusing combination of perfectly sanitized and abandoned. I guess the types of people who came to hotels like this didn't use the stairs.

A clacking of heels echoed above me. I dashed into the empty space in the middle of the square spiral staircase and looked up, hoping to catch a glimpse of the woman making her way up them. I couldn't spot her, so I hastened up the stairs as fast as I could, my grasp tight on the front of my dress as I sprinted up the steps. My breathing was heavy and I could feel the beginnings of blisters on both of my feet, but I pressed on. I picked up speed even though every muscle in my body begged me to do the opposite.

Another squeaking sound reverberated through the space as a door opened. The woman must have reached her floor. I hustled up another floor until I spotted the open door slowly closing, as if someone had just opened it. I slipped through, not wasting a second to push it wider, and rushed into the open hallway, dropping my skirt. To my left was nothing. When I turned to my right, I saw a figure, almost ghostly in her elegance, turning right down an adjoining hallway. I couldn't see her face, but I did spot a glimpse of red on her shoulder. *The pin,* I thought. *That's her.* And her hair, I'd seen her hair. Though she'd already turned out of sight, I was sure I'd seen it styled into a neat brown coiffure resting on her neck.

I stuck my hands into the sides of my dress fabric once again and lifted it, exposing my heels. I watched my feet move as I hurried down the hall as if in slow motion until I reached the hallway she'd gone down, only to see her turn onto another. It was as if she was an apparition, moving through the walls.

I found her, I thought. My brain tried to recollect a memory of a woman with brown hair in the tunnel, as if the small detail might trigger something deep within me. Nothing came. I pushed forward, feet cracking against the tiles as I moved to catch up with the woman I'd been looking for. The woman I'd forgotten. The woman who'd saved me so long ago.

Out of breath, I was forced to stop when I'd reached the beginning of the next hallway she'd turned down. But she'd stopped, too. Her back was to me, but I could tell she was looking down at something in her hands. Carefully, I slipped my shoes off and let them both dangle from my left hand, part of me nervous I'd scare her off if she knew I'd gotten too close. When I'd made it almost ten feet from her, I stopped again.

"What...what are you doing here?" I stammered, my words disjointed.

The woman turned around, her phone poised in her hand as if she was sending a message.

"Oh!" A hand went to her heart. "You scared me."

My heart was in my throat. I tried not to let my mind run wild, to make up scenarios for how this could be.

"*Mom?*" I whispered, looking her up and down. My mother stood before me, her brown hair tied into a chic low bun, her white slip dress making her look less like a mother and more like a debutante herself.

Pinned to her chest was the large ruby rose decorated with diamonds.

"Oh honey, I'm so sorry I'm late. I hope I didn't miss much. I was stuck in traffic for so long I really had to find a bathroom first before heading inside. You know I have a bladder the size of a pea. I tried the lobby bathrooms but they were too busy, I figured I'd try and find one near the ballroom and got a little lost." My mother took a few steps toward me, closing the physical distance between us but doing nothing to minimize the now gaping space that existed between us in my mind.

I didn't move toward her. "Where...your pin?" I asked, though I knew my question didn't make sense.

My mother raised an eyebrow, then looked down at her shoulder. "Oh, this? It's gorgeous, isn't it? It was your grandmother's." A wide grin spread across her face, and my world swirled before me.

My grandmother?

I searched for my voice. "Your mom?" I'd met my mom's parents a few times as a kid. They weren't super involved, nor did they care to be. And as far as I knew, neither of them had a connection to Rose Island.

She shook her head. "No, your other grandmother." She stuck her phone into the small purse dangling from her elbow that I hadn't noticed until now.

I didn't reply. I tried to conjure an image of a woman I'd never met in my brain, but I couldn't.

My mom walked over to me and rubbed my arm, obviously sensing my confusion. "Oh honey, I know we don't really talk about her. I'm sorry about that. It's just she left when you were a baby, and it upset your dad so much we couldn't really talk about it in front of you. Same for your grandfather, too. Before, I mean."

I flashed back to the tunnel, bouncing in someone's arms as they carried me down the dark path. "But mom, how long have you had that pin?" Had it been my own mother who'd saved me from the tunnel that night? Did she know more about the Order than she led on? I thought about the timing of my grandfather's death and our sudden move to New York, the way my parent's relationship fell apart after that. My father should have needed us more than ever after his death but instead, we left. Could my mother have been protecting me?

The rubies glinted in the harsh light of the hallway as my mother slipped her fingers over the pin and took it off, tilting the mix of gems toward me in her palm. "Well, when we moved to New York your father shipped us over a bunch of stuff. Some of his mother's things got mixed in, including her jewelry. I suspect your dad wants me to pass some of these things down to you. Which I will when you're old enough, of course."

My mind wandered back to the tunnel. No, it wasn't my mother that was there that night. She didn't have the pin yet. It must have been my grandmother. But if she'd disappeared when I was a baby, how could that be? She must have come to Newport, and to Rose Island specifically, for a reason. And for some reason I couldn't understand, she'd brought me.

But no, someone had worn the rose pin to my last debutante ball. Could my grandmother have come to see me then, to check up on me in secret? Except...

"I've never seen you wear it before," I said, hoping to elicit an answer to the question floating in my mind.

My mom looked up, thinking. "I've worn it before. You just didn't see it. I wore it to the last—"

"Debutante ball." I finished with her, closing my eyes.

"Harper, what's wrong?" My mother's voice was tinged with worry. "You're still embarrassed about that? I know it didn't go well last time, sweetie, but this is your chance to make up for it."

I let her words sink into the back of my mind. What bothered me wasn't the thought of my last ball, but the realization that our lead on this pin wasn't at all what we thought it was. My mom certainly did not have the information we were looking for. There was no source to swoop away to some foreign country, someone who could give us a lead on Malloy's treasure, the Fontaine will, or something, anything to take down the Order.

"Here." My mom bounced her hand up and down in front of me, the rose pin beckoning to me. "It's yours. I didn't know you'd like it so much."

I swallowed hard and slipped the pin from my mother's hand, letting its tough edges dig into the soft flesh of my palm.

"Alright, we should get going. I still have to use the ladies' room and you must be up soon." A warm

arm slipped around my shoulders and squeezed. "I'm so proud of you. I'm sorry I'm late, I hope I didn't miss much."

I forced a smile, but I knew it wouldn't reach my cheekbones. "No, you didn't. It's okay." I paused, attempting to force a clear thought into my brain. "I should go meet up with the others. You're right, we'll be on soon. I'll see you later."

I turned and headed back toward the elevators, unsure exactly where I was going—or of what would come next.

TWENTY-ONE

The elevator made quiet beeping noises as it swooshed from floor to floor. With shaking hands I grabbed my phone from its hiding place and texted my friends.

Found pin. Not what we thought. Disburse the fake pins.

I thought of the crappy counterfeit ruby broaches we'd had made at the last minute to try to throw off the Order, had they been smart enough to come to this event. An array of ruby pins, even if they were all slightly different from the rose pin, would be enough of a distraction to make Rebecca or the others question if they'd found the right person. And they had come, or at least Rebecca had, and now I was grateful we'd thought ahead. My mother, of all people, had been wearing the pin. That made her a target. And that was simply not an option.

The cold, smooth sensation of the rubies caressed my thumb as I ran it over the real pin, still in my hand. My mother had arrived late. The chances of her being seen by anyone Order-related was low, but certainly not zero. We may not have needed to fly her off to a different country, but we still needed to ensure no one found out she was the woman we'd been looking for. God knows what that would mean if they did.

My phone vibrated as a message came through from Nina.

Juicy. I'll find some guests to wear the fake-out pins without being seen.

And then, from Valentina,

Good. Now get back here. The introductions are starting soon and I think if the Order doesn't kill you, Mrs. P might.

Another vibration, followed by another message.

Sorry, too soon.

Not planning to piss Mrs. P off even further, I made it backstage just in time to line up with the rest of the debs. With their array of brightly colored dresses, the rich blues, sensual greens, and other jewel-tones, the sight was quite spectacular. I hadn't taken a moment to appreciate it earlier during the excitement of the dance but now, seeing everyone composed and all together, I appreciated, just for a moment, what this was all about.

"There you are!" V whispered, rushing up to me. "Mrs. P almost just killed me in your place, but she didn't have much of a choice but to agree to let me present you."

A grin spread across my face. "Well, it would look a little weird for us to disappear after the dance. People would talk." I tried not to be smug about it, but V's own smile told me she was pleased she would be the one to introduce me to the world as, as they say, a lady.

Suddenly everything I went through all those years ago at my last debutante ball was worth it for this moment.

"Ladies!" Mrs. P shouted, scurrying down the empty stretch of space beside the line we were making. "This is your moment! Just as we practiced, slowly and elegantly we will descend to the edge of the stairs. Your name will be called, along with your date's, and you will take his hand and make your way down slowly, allowing yourself to be presented as the precious butterfly you've become!" She noticed Valentina and I standing off to the side, and waved us into the middle of the line, mercifully far enough away from Little S and Edward that we wouldn't have to confront them.

"When you reach the bottom of the stairs, pose for a photo," she continued. "No hands on your hips or duck lips or any of the embarrassing unladylike things you've been taught to do these days." A couple snickers rang from the group, quickly silenced by a harsh look from Mrs. P.

The sound of music drifted in our direction from the hallway, causing a nervous tingle to shoot down my spine.

"This is it!" she shouted. "Let's go, and remember what I taught you!"

Moving as one, the entire group shifted down the hallway and through the entrance up a set of hidden stairs and onto the second floor. The music grew louder as the orchestra played across from us, each debutante careful to stick close to the wall so the guests downstairs wouldn't see us before our time. The setup reminded me of a theater or a concert hall, with the second floor wrapping around the open space in the middle like a balcony, but instead of stopping at the wall, both ends met at the regal looking stone staircase poised at the head of the room. The stairs displayed smooth gray stone and etched handrails, waiting to be graced by dainty footsteps. Musicians dressed in all black were placed across from the stairs on the far wall, tucked away as to not be seen and only heard.

But this was not a Broadway show or a concert. Tonight, we were the show. In two rows, with the ladies to the right and our dates to the left, we lined up at the top of the stairs, just as Mrs. P had instructed. Before we settled, I noticed Little S look over her shoulder from her place at the almost-front of the group with her new date, Edward, poised next to her. Her eyes flashed when she saw Valentina and me, making my heart drop into my stomach.

There was a hesitation, and then, before I knew what was happening, Little S guided Edward by the crook of his elbow out of the line, sliding covertly behind V and I. I met my girlfriend's eyes, a question lingering there. What was Little S doing? Mrs. P's voice boomed through loudspeakers as she began presenting debutantes, each pair following her instructions exactly and gliding down the stairs gracefully as they were presented.

"Good luck, Harper," Little S whispered over the announcements coming from the speakers. "You'll be *sure* to make *quite* the entrance." I looked back at her, allowing V to guide me forward as the line moved. Something in Little S's eyes made clear I *was* going to make an entrance, just not the kind I was planning.

V continued pressing me forward and I kept turning, paranoid to look away from Little S. I didn't know what she might do.

Until I did.

"Just be careful," she whispered again, as only three couples stood in front of Valentina and me. "I wouldn't want you to fall." A snicker fell from her mouth. "Or would I?"

"Harper," V's voice snapped me back to attention, the panic in her low voice signaling we had trouble far beyond falling down the stairs. "Do you hear that?"

I listened, the bellowing of our host's voice and clapping of guests filling the room. But then, faintly, a different sound filled the air. I gasped, the sound of clapping around me disappearing into the background. The distinguishable sound of whirring grew louder, the *whap-whap-whap* of helicopter blades ringing clearly to me now.

Someone was landing a helicopter on the hotel roof.

"Jack," Valentina and I whispered at the same time. He must have come back. Maybe he *did* care after all. He'd been sorry to leave. Was he sorry enough to come back for us? For the woman with the pin? She was a moot point by now, but he didn't know that.

Two couples were left in front of us, and Valentina and I were forced to step forward once more.

"If Jack is here," I breathed, "he's going to be caught. He must not know Rebecca is here. She probably has all kinds of Order people ready to take him." I leaned around the couples in front of me, just enough to spot Rebecca in the back of the room. Her chin was tilted up as she looked toward the ceiling, light brown pieces of hair falling regally around her face. A cell phone was cradled in her hand, as if she was about to text someone. "Rebecca looks like she's going to leave. She obviously knows Jack isn't here, at the actual ball. She must know something is up." I looked over at V, the alarm painted on her face mirroring my own. "We have to help him," I whispered.

V looked behind us for a split second. "We need to cause a distraction." Her voice was low, too low. We were talking about Little S, I realized. I glanced back at Little S myself, a devious look still playing at her lips. When I looked back at Valentina, her face was hard with resolve. "Get behind her. We have to do this quickly."

Only one debutante and her date were left ahead of us now, with the other couple posing for a photo at the base of the stairs. This was our chance. Before Little S could do anything about it, V pulled me by the arm, forcing us behind Little S and Edward the same way they'd done to us earlier, just as the pair in front of us began descending down the stairs. It was too late; if Little S tried to move now, the guests might see her.

This time, it was her looking over her shoulder at me with uncertainty in her eyes, matched with a strong dose of venom.

"Do it now," Valentina said to me, her eyes on the stairs, which were now empty and ready for the coming-out of the next two in line.

"Do what?"

"Introducing Shyla Patel, daughter of Padma Patel, sister of former debutante Shalene Patel, and introduced by Edward Belkin," Little S's mother boomed into the microphone, waving her daughter on with pride.

"This." Valentina's answer was as swift as her movement, with one stilettoed toe landing intentionally on the train of Little S's dress. Before I could react, Little S and Edward took a step forward. When she landed on the third step down, the dress finally met its resistance. Little S bounced back slightly, and Valentina removed her foot, the dress's train releasing down the stairs, just as Little S lost her balance, knocked into Edward and fell, rolling clumsily down the remaining four steps.

"V!" I shouted, my voice drowned out by the gasps and shouts of surprised, horrified guests. I couldn't see Shyla with the throng of people making their way around her. The crowd flashed before my eyes, morphing into wedding guests swarming my dad as he attempted CPR on my already dead friend.

"She was going to do it to you, Harper. Now, go. I'll make sure she's okay and then I'll follow you," Valentina said, pulling me back into the moment, her chin jutting in the direction of the exit. My attention, still slightly blurred by the flashback but rapidly clearing as adrenaline pumped through my veins, shifted to Rebecca out in the audience, who was standing now. She looked like she'd been heading out but was blocked by the chaos of many of the guests and employees now standing or rushing around, attempting to help but only further adding to the disarray.

With a final glance at V, I nodded and raced across the balcony. With my heart pounding, I slipped through one of the doorways and booked it to the stairs. The elevator wouldn't have roof access. In what felt like a repeat from earlier I rushed up what might have been hundreds of stairs, this time taking a second to rip my shoes off to ramp up my speed. Eventually I made it, spotting a door labeled *ROOF ACCESS*. With burning lungs I pushed open the door, a fierce gust of wind causing me to raise my hands in front of my face. My hair and dress flew wildly out behind me.

"Cunningham," I shouted at Jack, tiny rocks and dirt thwacking at the bare skin on my forearms. When I didn't get an immediate response, I lowered my arms slightly as the helicopter landed neatly onto the rooftop's landing pad.

My eyes jumped to the man inside the chopper. "Which one?" he asked, his gray hair coming into view.

"Allastair," I breathed, my words drowned out by the sounds of the wind.

But it wasn't the old man that scared me, it was the man in a black suit, similar to what Jack's bodyguards wore, that caused fear to prick all over my body, goosebumps rising on every inch of exposed flesh. Or more specifically, it was the gun he had pointed at me.

TWENTY-TWO

"Who is it?" Allastair yelled, his normally composed voice sounding much more fierce from the force it required to be heard over the harsh sounds of the helicopter blades cutting through the wind. I shook my head, not able to form words over the lump in my throat. The man beside Allastair held his gun steadily, the black tip pointed menacingly in my direction. I was close enough to turn and attempt to run back inside, but by fleeing I'd be sealing my own fate. Allastair would signal the man to shoot me dead. My best chance was to reason with Allastair.

"Being that my grandson has seemingly disappeared, I can only assume you found what you were looking for. Or should I say, whom you were looking for. Tell me. The rose pin. Who is the woman?"

They must think Jack was looking for the person the Order interrogated him about...that it was her, *the woman with the rose pin all along,* I realized. I couldn't let Allastair believe we really did know something. Because the truth was, until this week, we didn't. This had to be about Jack and what he went through, nothing more.

"Jack came to me," I said, the words spilling out of my jaw as it clattered nervously together. I was shaking. But I had to keep it cool. If I wasn't confident, there'd be no way in hell Allastair would buy what I was selling. "He was scared," I continued, keeping my eyes trained on the gray-haired man and not the faceless man beside him, his identity shielded by his weapon. "He came to us looking for help. But for whatever reason, he must have run scared."

One side of Allastair's mouth turned into a frown. "Then you know too much."

"No," I put up a hand. It was heavy and useless, but I did it anyway. "We—I—" I quickly covered, determined not to drag my friends into this. "I didn't feel like I had a choice but to help him. He was our chapter's leader. And...and I was concerned for Jack. Rebecca can vouch for that concern." The lie wasn't completely untrue. I had worried for Jack. But his grandfather didn't need to know the truth. Jack *was* gone. He'd ditched us, presumably to stay with the Matsudas to keep himself safe. And however badly he felt about that choice, it was all still at our expense. If I didn't throw him under the bus, it would be us falling to the fate he feared so much.

"It wasn't some big coup," I added. "It was just...him wanting to find out more. To understand."

The old man kept his gaze trained on me. After a moment, he spoke. "It's interesting that he needed to understand anything. As far as he was concerned, his focus should have been on school. Not the Order." So Allastair wasn't going to mention the brainwashing directly. He'd insinuated it happened, so that he and I could discuss it without ever admitting anything. There was a tiny part of Allastair that clearly didn't know how much I knew about the brainwashing. If that was the case, it was possible Allastair was in the dark about a lot of this after all. He must have wondered how Jack had broken the hold the Order had over his brain. He didn't know exactly who we were looking for or why.

If we were looking for answers, it almost didn't matter who we were searching for. And yet, there was someone Allastair had been interrogating Jack about before his brainwashing. It *was* someone they assumed I knew. I wondered for a brief moment if the woman really was the same person they'd been looking for. Whoever it was held the answers. Either way, they were looking for someone, and shortly after, we were too. But there were too many unknowns, too many possibilities. Allastair didn't like possibilities. I would have to use that to my advantage.

"I think something was wrong with Jack. He was all jumbled. I think that's why he was acting so weird." Let him believe his brainwashing went wrong. Let him think this is about Jack, not us.

"He was together enough to send you to one of our connections. Tell me why."

I bit my lip, then swallowed. "I don't know why."

Allastair squinted, then nodded at the gunman. "Do it."

My grandfather's falling body flashed before my eyes, blood splattering against the floorboards, the same words his longtime friend had just uttered echoing in my memory. He *would* do it.

Before I could protest, a body jumped in front of me. A pile of dark silky material shimmered before me as Valentina stepped directly in the shooter's path.

"Don't," V shouted, her arms going out to the side as if her spaghetti arms could block a bullet. But she was taller than me, and with her frame outsizing me in every way, I could no longer see Allastair or the man with the gun.

"It won't look good, will it?" she shouted, her throaty voice opposing the extra volume required to fight whooshing sounds of the wind. I stepped to the side just enough for the scene in front of us to come back into view. To my fervent relief, Allastair put up a hand, momentarily stalling the shooter. V continued, latching onto the momentum. "I don't know if the other Order leaders know exactly what you've been up to, but if an important Cunningham goes missing, right after his entire chapter dissolves, it'll look like the Order is crumbling. It'll look like *you* are failing. I know the Cunninghams run the Order, but you're not the only powerful family in charge. Maybe that won't be the case for long." My mind drifted to the six men with the gold rings at my induction ceremony last winter, Allastair Cunningham standing among them as only one of the group.

"How are you going to explain all of this to them without explaining everything else you've been doing? About the treasure." *And the brainwashing*, I thought to myself, silently punctuating Valentina's sentence the way I knew Allastair would as well. She didn't have to say it. It was entirely possible the rest of the Order didn't even know about their brainwashing trials. They certainly didn't know about the treasure, the Cunninghams have been looking for that themselves since the beginning. And having a weapon like brainwashing in their arsenal would give them even more leverage for a total takeover. V's assumption that they didn't know seemed to ring true, as Allastair continued his silence, processing the words of a desperate teenage girl.

V dropped her arms, relaxing as she finished her appeal to Allastair. "Now that your grandson is gone, you need Harper. You need us."

There was more silence, followed by a sudden laugh. Allastair's perfect teeth glinted, his mirth unfitting for the situation we were in. "What makes you think I couldn't simply evade the Order's questions with a little bit of misinformation? You forget, the Cunningham family has done just that for years, my girl. It's kept us exactly where we need to be. You overestimate your importance."

"And if word gets out that he's with the Matsudas?" I ask, stepping out from behind Valentina. She stuck her arm out to stop me from moving any closer. I grabbed it and slipped my hands into hers. Allastair's face fell instantly, and I knew I was onto something. Now, how to make my point without showing all of our cards?

"They're not exactly low profile." Valentina squeezed my hand, catching on to my point. "It might get out, you know. What will you do then?"

"As far as I've heard," I said. "His family doesn't like you much. I don't know why," *I did know why*. "But I'm guessing they're some sort of rival to the Order. I can't imagine what excuse you could come up with when the rest of the members get ahold of that information. Even you can't contain that kind of information for long."

The man's lips pressed together. "And you're saying if I bring you back to Newport and pretend the rest of the chapter is intact, it would distract from Jack's new alignment? You find yourself to be that consequential? Both of you?"

"Yes," V and I said together. We weren't simply hoping that was the case, we were banking our lives on it. This argument wasn't so different from the arrangement I'd made with Rebecca. She sought to get rid of me, to prevent me from poking around and discovering the kind of secrets the Cunninghams kept hidden. But it didn't work because Jack reappeared, throwing a wrench into her entire plan. Maybe she didn't know what her grandfather was planning for him, maybe she even thought they'd kill him, but his mere existence and now, his alignment with their adversary, changed everything.

"Harper and Jack were the only ones kicked out. I doubt you held a press conference to let them know about Harper a few months ago. Jack, maybe. But she could come back easily. She could join us." Valentina's words were almost ridiculous. Though I knew she was right about me, this idea that Valentina and the others were actively participating in the high school chapter was obviously untrue. This was a fact Rebecca was supposed to handle by finding someone new to lead the group, but clearly something she hadn't gotten around to establishing. With no one to lead them, it was as if it didn't exist. And with half the Order in New York this past week, it might as well not have.

But the hesitation on Allastair's face signaled our argument wouldn't be enough. He needed more than pretty words. He needed information. I had to give him something so he'd trust us, or at the very least deem us worthy of being brought back into a secure corner of his inner circle. Or even just his outer circle, either way.

"It was my grandmother." A fleeting pang of regret coursed through my veins and I offered up the single true piece of information in all this. If it was possible the jeweler did find out my grandmother was the true owner of the pin, Allastair would know. And if that was the case, this could prove to him we were on his side. Even if he didn't know, he was clearly looking for someone. Let my grandmother save me once more from all this.

I could see Valentina's attention turn to me out of my peripheral, but I kept my focus on Allastair. He tilted his head, eyebrows raising just slightly, as if this information surprised him. As if *I* surprised him.

"The woman Jack was looking for," I clarified, adding my own spin on it. "Was my grandmother. I never knew her. I didn't...I don't," I rephrased, "...even know what she has to do with anything. But she is the woman with the pin. I hope that helps you somehow." But it wouldn't, I was betting. Either she was already dead, or she was long gone. And everyone else who was connected to her and the mess they created—my own grandfather, and Adan Sr.—were dead. If she managed to disappear for over ten years, either the Order already found her, a thought I didn't want to linger too hard on, or their trail on her went cold. That is, assuming they'd been looking for her to begin with.

I didn't tell him I'd met the woman. If he learned about her connection to me in that tunnel, he would realize she'd come back when I was a kid, something I still didn't understand and hoped Allastair never would.

Because whatever secret she was keeping, it must have been big enough to risk coming back to Newport.

The offering was a dead end, but Allastair didn't know I knew that. I was praying this would be enough to prove to him that we were on his side, to convince him my exchange with Jack was not a rebellion against the Order at all, but an innocent happening.

I pictured Newport, with its lavish, pristine mansions and briny smell of saline wafting off the ocean waves. I thought of my dad, grieving a broken engagement alone. I conjured Jamie in my brain, and Adan, left behind. Adan, who'd told Valentina he had something to tell me, something he'd only tell me in person.

A lightbulb went off in my head. The gears turned round and round, pushing through the gritty feeling of wind and dirt flying at my skin. I knew who the woman with the rose pin was, and it had led to nothing. But Adan had something new for me, something I could only get by going back to my hometown. We hit a wall here in New York. We've been caught by the Order. And my mother now needs protecting. Which meant I needed to get away from her.

And I needed to get to Newport without being shot first.

I relaxed my face muscles, fighting for composure. I wouldn't make the same mistake twice. It was too late to keep my friends out of it now. "Don't kill me. Let us come back with you. All of us. We'll play house again, or whatever messed up secret society version there is. Just let us come home and we'll make things right. You've already lost so much."

A slow smile crept up Allastair's face, his soft skin wrinkling at the edges. "Just tell me one thing. What happened to the pin you were looking for? Did you find it?"

I paused, fighting to exchange a look with Valentina. She couldn't weigh in on any of this. She didn't know yet about my mom, and even the information about my grandmother must have been a surprise. I had to take the reins on this. I had to lie. But if there was any chance Allastair or his people saw my mother when she walked in the hotel wearing the pin, he'd know I was lying. I wondered momentarily if he was testing me. But no, he couldn't be, because his people would have swooped in and grabbed my mother the moment they spotted the pin if that were the case. Wouldn't they?

I took a chance. If he was still asking about the pin, he may want it for something. This couldn't just be about its owner. That meant I couldn't let him have it. "It's gone." A sad smile was forced across my face, as if the news crushed me. "According to my mother, the pin is long gone." I held his eyes with my own, begging him to believe me. With a single wave he could signal my death, this simple lie enough to confirm my treachery. I waited. V didn't move beside me, and I could swear she was holding her breath until finally, Allastair did wave at the man next to him. I let out the breath I realized I'd also been holding when the man lowered his weapon and sat back, relaxed.

A hand reached out of the helicopter in my direction, and it clicked that Allastair was beckoning me to him. A jolt of fear pulsed through my body, both from the acknowledgment that I'd gotten what I asked for—to be thrown back in Allastair's grasp—and also that he was expecting me to fly off in that thing. V's grip locked hard on my wrist, stopping me.

"We'll send for the rest of you," Allastair shouted at Valentina, and though his devious smile did nothing to comfort her, she reluctantly let go anyway. *No* would not be an acceptable answer. I took a step forward and hesitated, turning back to V and slipping my arms around her.

"I love you," I said in my normal voice, and the noise was swept away in the wind, almost like a whisper. Her arms wrapped tight around me, and I could feel the panicked fear in her touch.

"Be careful," she choked out. "If he doesn't come get us ASAP, I'm flying back to Newport myself to be with you. You will not be alone. I promise." In a careful maneuver, I stuck my hand in the folds of my dress, my hand wrapping around the hard edges of the rose pin. With my back still to Allastair, I wrapped my entire hand around it, and in a camouflaged move, slid the pin into Valentina's palm. I felt her tense beside me, but she knew what I was doing. I couldn't have the pin on me, not if I was going with Allastair. She'd have to hide the rose pin to conceal my lie from earlier.

When I was certain the item was hidden in her closed fist, I turned and walked the twenty feet to the helicopter, which was now hovering inches off the platform. My ribcage felt like it was shaking under the pounding of my heart, the gaping hole in the side of the machine not offering an ounce of comfort.

Allastair's hand reached down toward me once again and I took it. With surprising strength he pulled me up, my bare foot stepping distrustfully onto the step up, my heels long discarded somewhere in the stairwell. I felt a rush through my body as I was pulled inside and wedged between the Cunningham and his employee, neither of them hastening to buckle my seat belt for me despite the movement of the helicopter and my fluttering dress signaling we'd been lifted even further off the pad. I felt beneath me with shaking fingers, latching onto the rough strap of the seatbelt and pulling hard, struggling to clamp it tight around my waist.

When I finally secured myself, I dared a glance out the chopper, stomach dropping when I saw Valentina standing alone below us, growing smaller and smaller every second. Her dress billowed out around her and she did nothing to settle it, her face tipped up in our direction, watching solemnly as we flew farther away. I looked down at my own dress flapping in the wind around my ankles, my exposed feet biting cold from the sharp wind.

Allastair's voice was quieter now as he spoke, still loud enough to be heard over the boisterous noises of this contraption, but lower now that I was beside him. "I'm curious, Harper, what made you think I'd be interested to hear you out? I could have just shot you."

I swallowed, considering my words. Things may have worked out to this point, but I needed to remind Allastair why I was so important, why he needed me alive. Just in case. "I'm useful to you. If I wasn't, you would've killed me already." I thought of my family's connection to Malloy and the lost treasure. I was the heir to Malloy's fortune. If he killed me, he'd have to kill my father and every other Fontaine out there to remove our entire claim to the fortune—a fortune he's trying to keep hidden. Somehow, some way, our family must hold the secret to finding it. He's struggled to discover that key until now, and I was the missing piece. It's likely why he waited to kill my grandfather until he had no other choice—having a Fontaine as a pawn would become much more beneficial when the time came. As long as I proved to him I wasn't causing any real threat, I would be of much more use under his thumb.

He nodded, that sly smile still inched up the corners of his face. "It's too bad you're so resistant to all this, Harper. You would make a great addition to our family." I nearly choked on my own tongue at his statement. It felt so misplaced, amongst the threats and bartering for my life.

"What?" was all I could manage.

"With your instincts, your motivation despite the danger, you would make a great Cunningham."

I snorted, the humor at his statement pushing through the terror in the pit of my stomach. If I tried, I could briefly imagine Allastair as a regular old grandfather, chatting with me about his grandkids and arranging beneficial marriages like how I imagine regular wealthy families do. "Jack isn't really my type," I said, not stating the obvious.

"I meant Rebecca," he purred, as if the statement was the most obvious point he could make.

My lips parted in surprise. A chuckle fell from this throat. "It's the 21st century. Why would I, a smart

271

man, let anything other than strategy influence who may marry into my family? Power is power." He looked me up and down, but I knew he wasn't looking at my physical appearance. He was attempting to look inside me, to understand me further. "I've seen the way Rebecca treats you. She's fond of you. That's a great start." He pulled his phone from his pocket and read a message out of my view. "She's not pleased with me that you took her spot in this chopper, however, but I'll send her back with the others."

An image of Rebecca on the beach flickered through my vision, mixing the face of her grandfather with her own. The same calculating eyes bore into me that day as here in this tight space. *I really did see potential in you*, she'd said, and I could see that now in her grandfather's face as well. *I handled it my way so my grandfather wouldn't have to.* I considered the way her words implied she'd been protecting me. Maybe she had been. But then a flash of Dom's bloody corpse washed the thought away, leaving only hatred in its place.

"Rebecca is a murderer." My words were hard and watery, the memory of what she did to my best friend flooding any tiny cracks of affection for her that wormed their way into my brain.

"So was your grandfather. And your little girlfriend's father. We all are." The certainty behind his statement left a cold feeling in my gut. "And if you continue on this path, Harper, so too shall you be."

TWENTY-THREE

———◆–◆–◆———

Twelve hours. That's how long it had been since I left one home for the other. Valentina and Nina were indeed brought back to Newport on Allastair's command, just as he said they would be. There had been no interrogation, no pat-down. I'd simply been returned to my father's seaside estate, entirely within view from the Cunningham mansion. And that scared me more than a thorough frisking or lie detector test ever could. I didn't know exactly what Allastair, or even Rebecca, would be planning for me, but I knew what I had to do.

My feet crunched on brittling grass as I trudged over to the Vasquez house. Even if Allastair had drones on me, watching my every move, he couldn't possibly question a visit to my girlfriend's house. Valentina, though, was actually tucked away inside *my* bedroom, waiting patiently for my return and giving me the space I needed to talk to her brother. Or maybe, the space *she* needed. If I knew V like I thought I did, she was scared. Scared to hear whatever morsel of information was so significant it couldn't be expressed through text or phone. A secret that big threatened to shatter her world all over again, just as my admission of her father's hand in my grandfather's death had.

I breathed out, letting the air flow deeply into my body and out again. I had to approach this calmly. Being back at my house, at the very place where everything went down mere months ago, made the hairs on my arms stand on end. It didn't feel good. But leaving promptly following Dom's death had been the exact same thing my mom and I had done when my grandfather died. We ran. And all it did was leave me with gaps in my knowledge of this town and with even bigger questions than I'd have had if I'd stayed. I wouldn't make that mistake again. Maybe if we hadn't left, if we hadn't run from all the secrets and I'd been raised to know about my family and its history with the Order, maybe what happened to Nate wouldn't have happened to Dom. Because around here, the only things secrets bring are pain and death.

This town is where I'll find the truth. About my grandmother and my grandfather. About the Malloys. This is where it began, and this is where it has to end.

A melodious ringing sounded from inside the house as I pressed the doorbell, the heavy ocean waves crashing behind me under the nearby cliff. Instead of being soothing, it felt grievous, like anyone who touches the sea at this moment would be sucked in and lost forever. I refused to look back at the water, and at the silhouette of Rose Island tucked hazily behind the fog.

"Hola," the housekeeper greeted me with relative cheer. I told her I was there to see Adan and wondered briefly if she'd even let me see him. I know he wanted to talk to me, but he didn't know I was coming. From what Valentina had expressed, Adan didn't see anyone. Maybe this lady had been told to keep all guests away. She might even wave me off right now. But after a beat the door was opened wider and she welcomed me as I stepped inside.

When we made it to Adan's wing of the house, it had begun raining, and the pitter-patter of water mixing with thunder against the large windows. I was grateful I'd come when I did, but I hoped the weather wasn't some kind of bad omen.

Unfortunately, the sight of Adan's bedroom didn't offer me any optimism. The housekeeper and I stepped inside after a brief knock and no response. The blinds were closed, casting a dark shadow against everything in the room, the only light coming from a few table lamps placed strategically throughout the room. Adan was seated in a deep-set sofa facing away from the door, giving the impression of an old person living out their final days in a glum silence.

"Señor Vasquez, tiene visita," the housekeeper said in Adan's direction. There was no response, only the repetitive sound of rain beating against the windows. When he didn't respond, she spoke again, expectant. "It's Miss Harper Fontaine, señor." At the sound of my name, Adan's head jerked to the side, not quite looking at us but making his intentions clear.

"Gracias, Sofia," he said, his voice urgent as he shooed the woman from the room. She nodded and ducked out, closing the door behind her. The air felt stale, making it difficult to speak. Or maybe it was the tension in the room. Either way, I walked slowly around the long couch and wondered if it was okay to sit down.

"You can sit," he offered, not looking at me. I could see his face now, despite the dim lighting. He looked the same but somehow, older and more worn. I wondered if I looked different to him after all I'd been through too, knowing it wasn't time but the crushing weight of our experiences that have aged us.

I gulped as quietly as possible, wishing things could be as natural between us as they used to be. I took my seat on the edge of the couch, about four feet away from where he was sitting, and angled toward him.

"How…how are you?" I asked, my voice coming out a bit higher than usual.

"I know why you're here." His voice was low just like his sister's, but throatier than usual, like he wasn't used to using it.

"What is it, Adan?" I asked softly. Whatever it was, I needed to hear it. "Dom told me that day there was something I needed to know. Before he..." I swallowed again. "Before he died." I forced myself to say it, to normalize what happened to him in my brain. To accept it. Adan's eyes pressed shut and he leaned his head back against the plushy cushion of the couch. *Oh no, I was triggering him.* I myself knew exactly how that felt. I had to be careful or I might shut him down for good.

The thought grounded me. The very girl who could barely look her girlfriend in the eye a mere week ago was now sitting on the other side of the couch. Somehow, through all this, I'd begun healing. Maybe it was the thought of taking down the Order, or simply the rush of the hunt, but I was back on a path now I never imagined I would be.

"There was a voicemail," I continued, hoping to pull something from Adan. "Here, just listen." With all the emotional strength I could muster, I pulled out my phone and brought up my voicemails, scrolling past the messages left by my mother and girlfriend in the past couple of months to find the voicemail dated the day of my dad's wedding. With unsteady hands I pressed play, letting the tears slip uncontrollably from my eyes as Dom's voice floated through the air and into my ears for the first time since he'd left me this message.

I couldn't look at Adan, until I felt him tense beside me at something Dom said. *"Your grandfather's name was in the book like you said. I mean, it is in the book. But there's more. There's something else in here you need to see. I have to tell you in person. It's too big."* The recording stopped. Adan finally turned to me, slowly bringing his eyes to meet mine. His were also filled with tears.

"I didn't know about that message," he admitted, his voice shaky. "But I knew there was more. Not when it happened, I mean. I was a mess anyway; I don't think I could've put two and two together if I tried. Not with the arrest. They kept me there behind bars for a long time, Harper. Even though I'm pretty sure they weren't supposed to, legally even." *Rebecca,* I thought. She was proving her point to me. To us. That she was in control. "I didn't know what was going to happen. When they let me go, they gave me back all of my personal belongings. I didn't look at any of it for a long time. I even went to throw everything out— the clothes I'd been wearing that day, even my phone, I didn't want it." So that explains Valentina's frequent trips back to Rhode Island. Adan wasn't even checking his phone. He may not have spoken to her, but at least she could make sure he was okay if she came in person.

"But that's the thing, Harper. It wasn't my phone. I left my actual phone in here the day of the wedding by accident," he said, gesturing to the bedroom we were situated in. "After looking everywhere for the jewelry Valentina asked me to find, jewelry that didn't even exist, I found something else. I came back in here in a fluster and ended up leaving my phone behind. What I forgot about, probably repressed completely until I looked at it, was Dom's phone."

My breath hitched in my throat. "I discovered it when I left my house, on the way to the ceremony. I didn't recognize it, but it was an old model, so I figured it was probably Dom's. Plus, I could see he had about a dozen missed calls from you. That's when I knew something was up." I didn't interrupt Adan as he told the story, the timeline of events playing out in my mind just as it had thousands of times since it happened, but this time, filling in the blanks.

Adan let his face fall into his hands and rubbed his closed eyelids hard.

"Dom was smart. I don't know what you had him mixed up in exactly, but he knew whatever he was looking at was important. I know because when I turned his phone on after finding it again, I found a picture he took that day, probably minutes before his death. But something happened to him, and somehow his phone got lost in the mix. Whoever did this to him…the Order, I guess, from what V has told me, didn't find his phone because *I* already had. He must have dropped it in the scuffle, or running away or something."

My throat was dry, but I finished Adan's thought for him anyway, forcing out the words. "The police assumed the phone was yours when you were arrested. That's why no one knew you had it. Why no one could find it." I thought for a moment. "But why did you check Dom's phone? If you didn't want to deal with any of this anymore…why?"

"I didn't want to, but I had to make sure it was his." He looked down at his lap. "When I charged it and turned it on, the call log, the messages, everything was gone. Clearly the Order was able to do that somehow, I don't know how. But they didn't delete his photos."

"Dom doesn't have a cloud software," I whispered. "He can't afford it. His photos aren't synced to anything, they're only stored on his phone memory." I choked back what would have been a sob if I hadn't swallowed it. "We lost a lot of good photos to that stupid thing. Every time he lost it or it broke accidentally, we'd lose everything." A small, spiteful laugh escaped my lips, and I allowed my eyes to close, soaking this in. "But of course, not this time. This time, his pictures, they made it."

Wood slid against wood as Adan pulled open a drawer beside him. In the silence that followed, he pressed the *on* button on the side, and the screen lit up, brighter than ever.

"What was the photo," I asked, the circles he was talking in scaring me half to death. I knew he was about to show me, but I couldn't wait any longer.

"It was from a page in some kind of book. I recognized some of the names. And then I realized what it was," he explained, cutting a quick glance towards me. "It was a hit list. Just like Dom said in his voicemail to you. And…there was someone on it that you need to see."

"My grandfather," I started, but Adan cut me off.

"No, Harper. You don't understand—"

"Where is the ledger now?" I asked, interrupting him, the urgency in my voice clear as day. If Dom dropped his cell phone, maybe he'd dropped Allastair's precious ledger too. It was what got Dom and my grandfather into this mess in the first place. We thought we could use it to prove the Cunninghams' guilt, and maybe we still could.

"It wasn't with Dom's phone," Adan said, squashing my hopes. "I don't know where it is. The only thing like that I have...well, had seen...was a different hit list in Valentina's room. A little red book."

I could swear my heart stopped for a full minute. The red ledger was the list that Valentina and I found hidden in her dad's stuff days before the wedding. My grandfather and Valentina's dad had made it together, an almost accurate copy of the black leather-bound copy kept in Allastair's office. Of course the entries stopped when Nathaniel died, but it had been something. We thought it had been stolen by the Order.

"I found it the day of the wedding," Adan continued, and a note in his voice told me he was angry. "It was hidden in her room. I wasn't looking for it, but when she sent me on that wild goose chase to find jewelry that didn't exist, apparently to keep me away from the wedding, I found the ledger instead. That's when I first realized V had been keeping secrets from me. That you both had."

"Adan," I begged. "What did you do with it?"

A single tear slid down Adan's face. But by the clench of his jaw and hard fixation of his eyes set straight ahead, I knew it was a tear of rage. "I got rid of it. Threw it off the cliff. That's what I was doing when I found Dom's phone. I wanted to put an end to all of this for you. For all of us. It's the safest place for you. And if you look at what happened to me, you'll see that I was right."

I shook my head so hard my brain rattled inside my head, "You destroyed it? It could have helped us!" I tried to control my anger, but I couldn't help it. We were all complicit in this now, including Adan.

"You're not getting it, Harper. That wasn't what I had to tell you—"

"Adan, please, you don't understand the scale of what's going on here."

"The photo on Dom's phone, it's different from what was in the little red book you and V had. I know because I read it. There were more names on this list. A lot more. Some I recognized. And one I know you will too."

"But—"

"Just look for yourself." Adan opened the photo software on Dom's phone and pulled up an image, shoving the phone out to me. I paused, partially from confusion, and partially in preparation for what I might see.

It took a moment for the black ink scribbled on stark white paper to register. It was a list with the names of all the people the Order had killed over the years. This wasn't all of it, merely a fraction if anything. Clearly taken from somewhere toward the end of book, Dom had narrowed in on one particular section of the list. I scanned from the top down, trying desperately to recognize some of the names, but nothing stood out to me until I reached the bottom. *Nathaniel Fontaine.* My breath hitched, and I pressed my finger to the line on the page, as if the tiny screen was the real ledger, displayed open in front of me. Next to my grandfather's name was the date of his death, aligning perfectly with the year I turned six, and the very point in history in which Adan Vasquez Sr. shot him in the head. But there was something else very important about this entry.

It's too big. I don't know if you'll even believe me. Dom's words rattled in my head, the revelation of what he'd been trying to tell me hitting me harder than anything I've learned since I stepped foot back in Newport last year.

Next to the words *Nathaniel Fontaine,* where the year had once been written, was a thick, black line dragged intentionally across the date.

"It's crossed out," I whispered to myself. The date of death had been removed. Adan said nothing. I repeated myself, the meaning of this sending me spiraling. "It's...it's crossed out? It's crossed out." Finally sinking in, I jerked in Adan's direction, willing him to look at me.

"Your father didn't kill Nathaniel," I breathed. "My grandfather is still alive."

TWENTY-FOUR

———— ◆◆◆ ————

They faked his death, I thought, a sick peel of laughter expelling from my throat. *They faked his death,* I repeated over and over in my mind until I finally reached my grandfather's study, soaking wet from the rain. Despite the chill and tiny drops of rain, I felt nothing as I scurried down the path from Adan's house to mine. In a twisted parallel to the day I found Allastair's letter to Nathaniel, back when this all started the night after the induction ceremony, I burst into the room with a brand-new hunger for answers, this time exceeding mere curiosity. My fingers touched every surface, opening or moving anything that I could get my hands on in search of answers, so reminiscent of when I'd done the same thing last year.

It was all fake. It's the only thing that makes sense. Truly, it was. My grandfather was shot in the head, there is no way he could have survived. Which means, they faked it. Why would Mr. Vasquez have killed Nate after years of working together to bring the Order down? Without all the information, you could almost buy that Adan Sr. was a double agent, working against Nathaniel until the time came to take him out. Or maybe it was possible that killing Nathaniel was a necessary evil to keeping Mr. Vasquez in the Order's inner circle, perhaps something they'd even agreed upon in case one of them was caught to continue tearing the Order down undercover.

But knowing everything I know now, that just couldn't be. Adan Sr. was not a killer. And he certainly wouldn't have given my grandfather up to the Cunninghams. The only thing that truly makes sense deep in my soul is that Valentina and Adan's dad knew my grandfather had been caught and planned a fake death to get him out of there. And when the Order found out the truth somehow, the day they used a thick black pen to cross out the date of death in Allastair's ledger, *had* to be the day Allastair called for Adan Sr.'s death.

That's why he'd packed his bags, *that's* why he'd been planning a trip. Could he have been attempting to flee after being found out? Was he planning to meet someone, like my grandfather, or maybe…my grandmother?

My grandmother, I thought. The woman who'd saved me from the tunnel. Was she in on it? Had she come back from her own hiding to take my grandfather with her? Were they together now?

It was him, I realized. The person the Order interrogated Jack about, the very one they assumed we knew something about, and the person they seemed to think knew about Malloy's will. *They're looking for someone,* Jack had said during his hypnotism. It had been my grandfather that Allastair was looking for this entire time, not my grandmother. And somehow, they must have assumed the rose pin was a connection to him somehow, some small clue to finding the man who escaped with all their secrets.

Now, everything made sense. The hidden document proving Fontaine ownership of Rose Island confirmed my grandfather knew about our family's link to the treasure. If Allastair thought Nathaniel was looking for the will, he probably was. Maybe he even found it.

I looked around the study, the same perfectly organized space filled with books and mahogany furniture. The once dingy smell of cigar smoke that clung to the carpet was replaced mostly by a musty smell, probably from untouched literature and rarely maintained office supplies. I spun in circles a few times, seeing everything and nothing at all. The whole room spun, until my focus stopped on one thing in particular: my grandfather's ashes.

A simple yet obviously expensive blue urn sat ominously in the center of the bookshelf, surrounded by tales of adventure and tragedy. I wondered which my grandfather had succumbed to.

I reached toward the urn, my hands still damp from the rain, and touched its sides, taking in a deep breath to shake my nerves. I counted down to myself. *Three, two, one.* On one, I lifted the urn, but the weight was so much heavier than I was expecting I almost toppled over.

"Oh my god," I whispered, my eyes transfixed on the unknown sitting in my hands. "Are you in here or not?" I asked so quietly, I knew no one would hear me. Not even my grandfather, had he been listening from the beyond.

Finally finding my courage I reached for the lid, pulling hard.

It didn't budge.

"What?" I muttered, tucking the urn into the crook of my armpit and using my other arm to get some leverage. Still, nothing happened. I held it out in front of me and stared, every conversation I've ever had about my grandfather playing through my brain like a montage.

"No," I shook my head. "You're not really dead, are you?"

With that I lifted the cumbersome vase in the air and promptly released it, the smooth touch of the urns glaze slipping easily through my fingers. The urn dropped five feet from where I'd held it as if in slow motion, taking its time before finally crashing to the oriental rug and splitting open with a hard crack that sent ceramic shards in every direction.

My arms shot up to cover my face, much like they'd done less than a day ago when Allastair had landed his helicopter on the roof. The sprinkling of a fine, grainy substance dispersed all over the room, covering my damp arms and settling into piles on the floor.

"No," I whispered, lowering my arms slowly, not wanting to see what I'd just done. I did something I could never take back. How would I explain to my father how I'd thrown his own father's ashes all over the room like it was nothing?

"Wait," I whispered, dropping to my knees. I looked down at the ground, then lifted my arms, turning them round and round to examine closely the substance pressed uncomfortably against my skin.

Sand.

My grandfather was alive. Sitting in this urn for over ten years was nothing but a pile of *sand*.

I stuck my hand into the pile in the middle of the room, careful not to cut myself on stray shards of broken ceramics, but desperate enough to confirm what my eyes were telling me. The cold, hard feel of the tiny grains of sand verified what my brain was screaming. This was not ash. My grandfather had never been inside that vase. But something else certainly had been.

Something cold and metal met my fingers and I froze, thinking back to the bullet casing found at the Rose Island Lighthouse. That bullet had never truly hit my grandfather's skull, that much had to be true. It was either a clue left behind for someone, maybe even me, or the leftovers of a gunshot released just far enough away from my grandfather's head to look real. Either way, the item beneath my grasp right now wasn't that.

I pulled the item out and held it in the air, a glint of silver reflecting in the light. It was a key. The number 38 was etched on one side. A keychain dangled from the metal, the tiny rectangle housing a colorful painting of a boat much like the one my grandfather owned and Dom had restored this summer. The very same where I found the old document proving the Fontaines owned Rose Island. I flipped it over. On the other side of the key was more etching, a string of numbers too long to mean anything to me.

I stood up and dusted the sand off myself as best as I could, though the act was futile, then walked over to the window overlooking the Rose Island Lighthouse.

"You left me a clue," I said, my words bouncing off the window, their meaning sitting deep inside me. "You're alive. After all this, you're really alive." I spoke to my grandfather, hoping one day to say all this to his face. But in the meantime, there was at least one person I could say it to, and she was waiting patiently in the other room. Leaving the sandy mess behind, I bounded out the door and down a string of hallways until I reached my bedroom. The familiarity of the space shook me every time I stepped inside, reminding me that Newport had, in fact, become home to me. I didn't realize it until I'd left, but I'd really missed it here.

"Valentina." My hands went to my knees as I caught my breath. Her dark hair whipped across her shoulders as she looked at me, dropping the book in her lap. The chair squeaked as she stood up, rushing over to me.

"What is it?" She looked me up and down, her brows pinching as she examined me soaking wet with sand clinging to my skin.

"I don't even know where to start," I said, holding up the tiny metal key and mysterious keychain. I wasn't talking about just the key, but it didn't matter, V had already narrowed in on it. Her grip held onto the bottom of it, turning it this way and that, examining all of its sides.

"I do," she said, a smile turning up her face. "I may not know what this is all about yet, but I know what this goes to." She pointed to the long string of numbers I hadn't been able to make sense of.

"Call Nina. I'm driving."

TWENTY-FIVE

The jingling of keys reverberated off the walls as a bank teller marched toward a room filled with shiny metal boxes, each labeled with its own number. There were hundreds of them. The room was located on a lower level I hadn't been aware Newport Bank had even had. Not that I'd spent much time here before today anyway, but still.

"Well ladies, here we are," the teller said, stopping in front of a safety deposit box numbered 38. Her ashy hair was slicked into a perfect bun to match her cliche pencil skirt. We watched the woman show off her manicured nails as she selected a key off a keyring and unlocked the chamber, sliding a long rectangular box from the hole and placing it on the matching metal table in the center of the tight space. We'd shown her our own key, but apparently she didn't need it.

"I'll leave you to it. When you're finished, you may put the box away securely and let me know." The classy clicking of heels faded in the distance as she made her way to the main floor, leaving Nina, Valentina and I alone with the closed box.

"Okay," I shrugged. "Let's see what my grandfather left in here."

"Uh, are we sure Allastair or his cronies didn't like, follow us here?" Nina squeaked, looking over her shoulder as if the man himself would appear.

Valentina placed her hand on Nina's shoulder. "Don't worry, it's just a bank. Most of our families have money here. It's not suspicious. If he's going to see us go anywhere, this is the last place I'd worry about. Plus, if he had any indication Nathaniel was hiding something here, he'd have already gotten to it one way or another."

My eyes dropped to the shiny box in front of me. "He couldn't have, could he?" I asked, raising an eyebrow at my friends. "He'd need the key, he'd need to know the number…he'd need to know about it to begin with…right?" I didn't like how tight my voice sounded.

"There's only one way to find out," Valentina offered, nodding at the box.

I pressed my fingers to the cold metal and breathed in. V and Nina watched with bated breath as I pulled the top open. Something was inside. *Something was inside!* Okay, so barring a "you're too late" message from the Cunninghams, chances are high whatever this is is what my grandfather meant for me to find.

I let the metal top drop all the way to the table, the harsh fluorescent light pouring over its contents, revealing a colorful piece of paper tucked neatly inside. Valentina pressed tight against my side, leaning in to see what I was looking at.

"Me too!" Nina shouted, smushing herself against my other side. "Is that?"

"A map?" I finished for her, pulling the thick folded paper from inside and laying it flat on the table. With quick hands I unfolded the picture, revealing what was indeed a hand-drawn map of part of an island. Was this Rose Island? It couldn't be, Rose Island was much smaller than this plot of land showed.

"It's an island," Valentina surmised just as I had, pointing to the water surrounding the majority of the coastline. "But it looks like it's just one corner of it." Multiple streets intertwined on the page, little squares marked with numbers scattered along them, probably indicating house numbers.

"Awesome!" Nina chirped. "But, what's the significance?" She leaned in, reading the name etched into the top of the paper in small writing. "*Bishop's Cove.* Huh. Sounds familiar."

"That's so weird," I said, scanning the entire document from top to bottom. "Is my grandfather trying to tell me he's hiding somewhere on this island? At...Bishop's Cove?"

Nina stuck her pinky in her mouth and gnawed on a hangnail. "Well, a map *is* a pretty good clue. But it's not much to work with. Is that all that's in there?"

I stuck my hand in the box and pressed it to every surface only to find it empty. "Yeah. All we have is the map and the key." I pulled the key from my pocket and threw it onto the center of the map.

"Hmm," Valentina ran her fingers through her glossy hair. "What's with the keychain?"

We all leaned in. "Well, you'd need a boat to get to the island, could that be what he's saying?" Nina offered, poking at the boat painting on the keychain and sliding it absentmindedly until the name of the street on the map below was exposed.

"Wait!" I pressed my pointer finger hard to the street name. "Primrose." Valentina and Nina looked confused, matching frowns looking up at me. "Primrose," I repeated, and pointed to the boat pictured on the keychain. "My grandfather's boat, the one my dad never got rid of, it's named Primrose."

"Hold on," Valentina said, flipping the key over. "This could be a shot in the dark, but the key is number 38. Is there a 38 Primrose Street, or Primrose Ave or something? Maybe he's been working on this for a long time, trying to send you a message."

We all scanned the thick paper for the number, but Nina spoke first..

"Ooh, got it!" Nina yelled, and I shushed her, even though no one was around. "There. 38 Primrose Lane. I think V is right, maybe he's leading us to this address."

I scratched my head, thinking. My feet pulled around the room, pacing in circles as I considered this.

"Is this too easy? Would Nathaniel really leave clues to point directly to him? What if the Order really did find this first?" Valentina asked, voicing exactly what I'd been thinking.

"Maybe you need the compass first," Nina offered, and V and I whirled around to see Nina holding up the map of Bishop's Cove.

"What compass?" I asked, eyes wide.

"This compass," she said, flipping the map over to reveal a completely white backside, bearing only the words *Rose + Compass*.

"Ah, fuck," V cursed, putting her hands the sides of her face. "What are we supposed to do with a compass? Use it to find the island? Or something else?" she asked, and Nina and I fell silent, neither of us knowing the answer. I considered this.

"We have the boat, we have the location." I slipped my hands into my jean pockets to find my new favorite collector's item. The rose pin tumbled around in my hand, landing flat on its back. "We have the rose." I pulled up my sleeve, revealing the compass tattoo with the rose placed strategically inside inked onto my arm. I hovered the pin over the illustration, matching it up over the compass. "I guess there's only one thing left." I looked up at my friends, their intense gazes yearning for answers as clearly as my own was.

"Where do we start?"

BOOKS BY THIS AUTHOR

ROSE + COMPASS SERIES

There Can Only Be Six (Book 1)

There Can Only Be Blood (Book 2)

There Can Only Be Secrets (Book 3)

ABOUT THE AUTHOR

Follow Andrea on Instagram at @ani.levesque and check
out her website at www.andrea-levesque.com.

If you enjoyed this book, please consider leaving a review!